W9-CMD-422

PREGNANT ON THE EARL'S DOORSTEP

PREGNANT ON THE EARL'S DOORSTEP

SOPHIE PEMBROKE

MILLS & BOON

First published in Great Britain 2019
by Mills & Boon, an imprint of HarperCollins*Publishers*
1 London Bridge Street, London, SE1 9GF

Large Print edition 2019

© 2019 Sophie Pembroke

ISBN: 978-0-263-08302-6

MIX
Paper from
responsible sources
FSC™ C007454

This book is produced from independently certified
FSC™ paper to ensure responsible forest management. For
more information visit www.harpercollins.co.uk/green.

Printed and bound in Great Britain
by CPI Group (UK) Ltd, Croydon, CR0 4YY

For Carolyn

CHAPTER ONE

LENGROTH CASTLE LOOKED bigger than it had on the website. More imposing.

On the slick, professional website of the Earl of Lengroth the castle had been bathed in sunlight, with impossibly blue skies shining behind its corner towers, the stone walls almost white in the sunshine. In reality, even on a dry July day in Scotland, the skies were more white with cloud than blue, and the stone was a heavy, dark and imposing grey. The seventeen stone steps up to the dark wooden front door seemed designed to put visitors off altogether—they were narrow, steep, and they looked slippery with moss encouraged by the moat they rose across.

In fact, the whole scene was enough to make Heather Reid want to jump on the first train back to Hertfordshire and never return.

Except she couldn't. Not until she'd done

what she'd come to do. After that…? Well, what happened next was anybody's guess. By then the ball would be firmly in the court of Ross Bryce, Earl of Lengroth.

Steeling herself, Heather crossed the gravelled courtyard from the open front gate and carefully made her way up those seventeen slippery steps. Halfway up, she risked a glance down at the moat. The water was black and bottomless. Much like her fear.

Heather swallowed and took another step.

A splash beside her made her jump and almost lose her footing. Grappling for purchase on one of the higher steps, Heather darted her gaze around, looking for the cause of the sound. A fish? Duck? Crocodile? She wouldn't put it past the Earls of Lengroth to have installed the Loch Ness Monster in their moat.

Then she spotted the rubber duck, bobbing happily on the dark water.

'Not a monster,' she whispered to herself. 'That's a start.'

But that duck definitely hadn't been there when she'd started climbing the steps. Risking letting go of her step, Heather looked up at the windows overhead, trying to see who might have thrown the rubber duck.

Nothing.

Ross Bryce had kids, she remembered uncomfortably. Two of them, perfectly turned out in a party dress and a sailor suit respectively, featured on the home page of the website, standing and smiling sweetly next to their handsome father, the Earl, and their beautiful mother, Lady Jane Bryce, Countess of Lengroth.

She'd been physically sick when she'd seen that photo and realised how monumentally she'd screwed up. Of course, she'd been throwing up a lot lately anyway. But seeing that photo had marked the moment she'd realised just how much trouble she was in, and the magnitude of the consequences she had to face.

There was still no sign of the duck's owner, but Heather had been a teacher long enough to know that when a child threw a duck at you it meant you weren't wanted. In fact, she was pretty sure she'd have been able to figure that much out even *without* her teaching qualification.

Carefully, she reached down to the water and retrieved the duck as it bobbed past, tucking it under her arm.

'I don't want to be here, either, kid, believe me,' she muttered.

And then she took the next step anyway—because what choice did she have?

She'd made a mistake and now she needed to own up to it, deal with it and face it head-on. She knew only too well what happened when people ducked their own guilt and tried to cover up their actions with lies.

The big brass knocker on the castle door echoed around the courtyard as she lifted it and let it fall against the wood. At least she'd survived the steps and the duck missile. As long as the door didn't open outwards and send her flying into the moat she was almost there.

And then would come the really hard part.

She'd practised what she would say to Ross—it was hard to think of him as the Earl of Lengroth at this point—all the way up on the train. She'd thought of different ways to break the news, but it all came down to the one basic fact.

I'm pregnant. With your child.

She really hoped his wife wasn't in the room when she saw him again.

Not that he'd mentioned his wife, of course, when they'd met that night in London. Or his kids. He'd told her about the castle, and about lonely dark Scottish nights—even in early June, apparently. He'd talked about the countryside and his responsibilities and the parties he went to.

But he'd failed to mention his family. And he hadn't been wearing the wedding ring she'd seen on his finger later, in the most prominent website photo of them all—a large family portrait.

'You must have all the aristocratic ladies after you,' she'd joked, when he'd told her where he lived and shown her a snapshot on his phone. *'How do you know they're interested in you and not your castle?'*

'Trust me,' he'd replied with a wicked grin. *'My castle is the least impressive thing about me.'*

Heather groaned, just remembering the line. How had she fallen for that? She blamed the cocktails her friend Lacey had insisted on them drinking.

Was anybody *ever* going to open this door? She really wasn't enjoying reliving the worst mistake of her life in her head while she waited. She'd done enough of that over the last month as it was.

Now she was there, at Castle Lengroth, she just wanted to get this over with. She wanted to see Ross Bryce and tell him everything. She wanted this to be someone else's problem, too, even if just for a few minutes before he inevitably threw her out.

Heather didn't have high hopes for this meeting. But she knew it was something she had to do. Ross deserved to know about the baby— even if he didn't want anything to do with it, or her, after this. At least she'd have done the right thing.

Because, apart from one stupid night in London almost two months ago, Heather Reid *always* did the right thing. Her mother had taught her that much—if only by being a stunning example of what happened when a person didn't.

Finally the door creaked open to reveal an elegant, polished older lady in a navy skirt suit and a cream blouse, with a string of pearls around her neck and sensible navy shoes on her feet.

'I'm here to see the Earl of Lengroth,' Heather said as confidently as she could, as if it were the sort of thing she said every day.

'You're late,' the woman told Heather sternly. 'Come on. He's waiting.'

Heather blinked twice, then followed. She got the feeling that this woman wasn't used to being disobeyed.

'Um…how am I late, exactly?'

Well, she *was* late—six weeks late at this point—but she was pretty sure the woman wasn't talking about Heather's period.

'I didn't have an appointment…' Maybe she should have made one. Except she couldn't imagine that Ross was going to be happy to see her again.

The woman didn't answer—in fact, Heather wasn't even sure if she heard her over the sound of her own heavy footsteps on the polished stone floors of the hallway. On either side the walls were painted dark shades of green, in between bare stone columns, and every now and again they'd pass a chair with tartan cushions, as if there to give people a chance to recover from the unrelenting hard darkness of the place.

Finally, after several more hallways, eight chairs and two staircases, the woman stopped in front of another heavy wooden door and rapped her knuckles sharply against it.

'Come in,' a male voice called, and as the woman opened the door Heather thought she heard him mutter, 'Finally...' under his breath.

Heather stepped inside just as the woman said, 'The new nanny is here, sir.'

Nanny? Okay, someone had got something *seriously* confused here.

But as Heather stared at the darkly handsome man behind the mahogany desk she realised that a case of mistaken identity was the least of her problems. Because the man sitting at the desk belonging to the Earl of Lengroth wasn't the man she'd slept with in London almost two months earlier.

Cal Bryce had never harboured any ambitions to be the Earl of Lengroth. He didn't want the title, the castle, the requirement to provide an heir, the responsibility, or to have to uphold the reputation expected of a sterling member of the aristocracy.

And in fairness, he still didn't have most of those things. He wasn't the Earl—he remained the Hon Calvin Bryce, as he'd always been as the Earl's younger brother. The castle *wasn't* his—it belonged to his nephew Ryan, the eight-year-old newly minted Earl. He *didn't* have to provide an heir—and he didn't think anyone was expecting Ryan to do so for quite some years yet.

Since his brother Ross's death, however, the responsibility *was* all his—at least until Ryan turned eighteen. And the reputation... Well, it seemed that was Cal's to fix, too.

What on earth made you take that corner so fast, brother? Cal thought, not for the first time since he'd got that middle-of-the-night call and heard Mrs Peterson, the castle housekeeper, shrieking incomprehensibly down the phone at him from thousands of miles away in Scotland.

'They're dead! They're both dead, Cal!' she'd finally managed to say.

And the bottom had fallen out of Cal's world.

His whole life Ross had been a constant. And he'd needed that so badly—especially when they were growing up. While the world around them might have believed that the Bryce family were a perfect example of modern aristocracy done right, Ross and Cal had known the truth.

The family weren't above scandal and outrageous behaviour—they'd just grown very, very good at covering it up.

As a child, all Cal had known was that he had to get out of the way when his father started shouting, and that if he was drinking it was better not to be in the castle at all. Ross, three years older, had taught him all the best hiding places—and the signs to look out for telling him that it was time to run. And when Cal got it wrong Ross had stood between him and the Earl to give his little brother a head start.

Cal had idolised Ross. Until six weeks ago.

Even as he'd grown up into a teen, and then a young man, it had taken Cal some time to realise the true nature of his genetic inheritance. The Bryces hid their scandals well—even from their own flesh and blood. But once he'd seen his first evidence—walking in on his father in bed with the barmaid from the village pub was a scene sadly seared into his memory— he'd started to notice it everywhere. Especially as his parents had become less careful of their words around him.

There was the affair his mother had been having with the family lawyer for most of Cal's life. The endless parade of barmaids and local girls he'd seen letting themselves out of the castle kitchens in the mornings. The bruises on Ross's face and arms after a shouting match with their big bear of a father—red-faced and fuming so much of the time.

Hell, there was even the legend of the Lengroth ghost, which was currently causing him issues in ways the woman couldn't possibly have imagined a hundred years ago when she'd died. The story went that a century earlier one of the local village girls had got pregnant and claimed the father was the Earl. Shunned by the local village people, and with her reputation ruined, she'd come to the castle to ask for his help. The Earl had denied her and sent her away, and she'd fallen down the castle steps and died—although some still whispered to this day that she'd been pushed.

Cal wished he didn't know the truth about that one, if he was honest. His ancestors were enough of a disappointment to him already.

But not Ross. Ross had married the beautiful and lovely Janey and had two beautiful and lovely children. Ross had bucked the family trend.

Cal couldn't even look at the battlements of Lengroth Castle without remembering all the awfulness that had happened inside it. But Ross had moved the family in—made the castle a home, even if it *was* still stone-walled and imposing. Ross had found a way to overcome their genetic disposition towards scandal and bad behaviour.

At least so Cal had believed, until he'd returned home to take over the reins after Ross's death.

Now he was starting to think that Ross had just been better than all of them at hiding his true self.

Cal had thought that the world of business was hard—building up and running a company with a multiple seven-figure turnover took time, energy and commitment. He'd thought he understood about responsibility and challenges.

But that had been before he'd had to deal with the gambling debts, the lies and promises Ross had left behind him.

And before he'd had to hire a nanny for two grieving and uncontrollable children.

He eyed the latest one—the ninth in six weeks—as Mrs Peterson showed her in. In addition to being a full forty minutes late, she looked a little casual for a job interview, dressed in a flowery sundress and sandals— with a jumper on top because this *was* summer in Scotland, after all. Her copper-coloured hair flowed loose in waves over her shoulders, and she carried a rucksack on her back, as if she were a gap year student going travelling. Which she might be, he supposed. She looked young enough.

She also had a rubber duck tucked under her arm, but Cal decided he wasn't even going to ask about that.

The bottom line was that desperate guardians couldn't be choosers, and the agency must be running out of nannies to send him by now.

Mrs Peterson was also looking unimpressed with her. *She*, Cal noticed, was wearing her best suit and heels—the way she always did when there was a potential new member of staff on-site or an important visitor of some sort. She must have got more wear out of it in the last six weeks than in the decade beforehand. But Cal knew she'd have her fluffy slipper boots back on the moment she made it back to the kitchen. The stone floors of Castle Lengroth were hard on the feet.

He turned his attention back to the nanny. Part of him wanted to dismiss her out of hand, but another, larger part, knew that he needed her. He wasn't capable of being the parental figure his niece and nephew so desperately required. He just wasn't father material—he'd always known that.

Which meant he needed someone who would stick it out and look after Daisy and Ryan for the next six weeks—and he'd got the impression from his most recent call to the agency that this was his last shot.

Which meant he had to be persuasive. And he had to follow the plan he and Mrs Peterson had cooked up the night before.

1. Offer her more than she can get any-where else

2. Make it completely conditional on her finishing the six weeks

3. Don't mention the ghost

Easy.

'Okay, Miss...' he consulted the notes from his call with the agency '... Thomas. Here's the deal. My niece and nephew need a reliable, effective and capable nanny for the next six weeks of the school holidays, until they leave for boarding school in England. Your agency says that you're up to the job, and I have to believe them. So I'm going to make you an offer you won't get anywhere else. If you stick out six weeks here at Castle Lengroth, and get the children prepared physically, mentally and emotionally for boarding school, I'll pay you for a full year's work at your agency base rate. But if you quit before the six weeks are up you get nothing.'

The redheaded nanny opened her mouth, then closed it again. Then she said, 'I think there's been some sort of misunderstanding—'

Cal cut her off before she could get any further. That was another thing he and Mrs Peterson had agreed on—not giving her too much time to overthink things. He knew that the agency nannies talked to each other—they probably had their own message group on social media or something—so she almost certainly already knew the situation here.

The last nanny had quit before she'd even made it into the castle, when ten-year-old Daisy had thrown a bucket of soapy water over her from the nursery window above the front steps. Cal wasn't risking losing this one before she even met the devil children.

'I know what you must have heard from your predecessors, Miss Thomas,' he said, smiling as charmingly as he could, given what was on the line here. 'I can't imagine it's many families that go through eight nannies before they find the right one. But I have an excellent feeling about you,' he lied.

'Eight nannies?' she echoed faintly, and Cal

cursed himself for mentioning it. It sounded so much worse spelt out like that.

'The children have been through a lot since their parents died nearly two months ago,' he said, defensively. 'It's natural that they're acting out a bit. And, in fairness, seven of the eight said it wasn't the children that drove them away, it was the ghost.'

Dammit. I wasn't supposed to mention the ghost.

In the doorway, Cal saw Mrs Peterson throw up her hands in despair and turn to leave, closing the door behind her. Obviously she knew a lost cause when she saw one.

But the new nanny didn't even seem to register his mention of a supposed supernatural being haunting the castle. Probably because she was a sensible person who didn't believe in ghosts and was going to accept his offer. He hoped.

'Eight nannies in less than two months?' she said incredulously.

Then her pale face turned somehow even whiter. Cal resisted the impulse to check over his shoulder for the ghost.

'Wait, their parents…? The Earl of Lengroth, Ross Bryce, and his wife…?'

'Yes. My brother, Ross, and my sister-in-law, Janey,' Cal confirmed, confused.

She sank into the chair opposite him without being invited to do so. Since she looked as if she might fall over otherwise, Cal didn't object. He probably should have asked her to sit before he'd hit her with the terms of the job, actually.

'They died? When?'

She placed the rubber duck on the desk absently. Really—*who* brought a rubber duck to a job interview?

'Almost two months ago,' Cal repeated, since the information clearly wasn't going in.

She couldn't be a local girl if she didn't know that already, although he'd guessed that from her accent anyway. It had been a mere blip of a mention in the national news—a blink-and-you'd-miss-it piece. But locally it had dominated the newspapers for weeks.

'June,' she said softly, and bit down on her lip. 'It must have been just after I—' She broke off and shook her head, copper curls rustling.

'Miss Thomas. Tragic though my brother's

passing is…' Cal swallowed hard at the memory, hearing Mrs Peterson's panicked voice all over again '… I really think we should get back to the matter in hand. Your position as nanny to my niece and nephew.'

She looked up, her green eyes bright. 'And *I* think, Mr Bryce, that we need to start over. You see, I'm not Miss Thomas from the agency, and I'm not here for the nanny position. I'm here about your brother.'

And suddenly Cal knew that his faith in his perfect older brother was about to take another hit.

One it might not be able to recover from.

CHAPTER TWO

THE YOUNGER, EVEN more handsome Bryce brother stared at her across the desk—some sort of family heirloom, Heather supposed, given the weight and colour of it. The rubber duck clashed horribly with the surroundings, bringing a sense of surrealism to the whole scene.

As if it wasn't absurd enough already.

Don't get distracted by the desk. Or the duck. Focus on what you're here to do.

Except mentally debating the provenance of furniture was far easier than telling the man sitting behind it that she'd had a one-night stand with his dead brother. Before he was dead. Obviously.

Oh, this was going to go badly.

'You're not from the agency?' Mr Bryce repeated. 'Then who exactly are you? And, more importantly, who were you to my brother?'

Did he already know? Maybe Ross had done this sort of thing all the time. Maybe she was just the latest in a line of women his brother had taken 'meetings' with over the last couple of months.

Heather took a deep breath, and began. 'My name is Heather Reid,' she said, forcing herself to meet his gaze. 'About two months ago I met your brother, Ross, in a nightclub in London and spent the night with him. And now I'm pregnant with his child.'

A child who would never know their father. Heather clutched at the arm of the chair as reality hit home now the words were out in the open. Ross was dead. The vibrant, laughing, charming man she'd spent the night with was gone. More importantly, her child's father was dead.

He might have been an adulterous liar, but she wouldn't wish death on *anybody*. Especially since it meant she was all alone in this now.

Even if Ross had thrown her out of the castle she'd have always known that her child had a father he or she could go to later, if they needed to. That there was someone else in the world that they belonged to.

And now there was only her. And her baby's uncle, sitting on the other side of that damn desk, staring at the rubber duck she'd placed between them.

His expression had hardly changed, she realised. Whatever he was feeling about her revelation, it wasn't shock. Which told her a lot more about Ross's general behaviour than she liked.

'Mr Bryce?' she said, when he didn't answer.

'Cal,' he said tiredly, rubbing a hand over his forehead. 'My name is Cal Bryce.'

'Right. Um… Cal, then.' She waited. Still no response. 'Do you want to… I don't know…see some ID or something?'

Cal's eyebrows rose slowly as he turned his gaze back on her. 'For you or for the baby?'

Heat flushed to her cheeks. 'Right. Obviously you'll want some sort of DNA test at some point—which is fine. I mean, for all you know I'm some random woman who read about your brother's death and came here to try it on and get some money out of you. Except I'm not.'

Cal was looking at her as if that was *exactly* what he thought she was, now she came to mention it. Heather couldn't really blame him. She was *not* good at this.

'Oh! I have one thing that might help...' She pulled her phone from the pocket of her dress and scrolled back through the photos to find the one she wanted before holding it out over the desk to show him.

His eyes darkened as he stared at the photo of her and Ross, surrounded by the dim lights and noise of that London bar, both grinning into the lens as he'd held the phone out to snap the picture. Something to remember him by, he'd said.

Turned out she really didn't need the photo.

Cal sat back, looking up again, over her shoulder, and Heather took the phone back. This couldn't be pleasant for him, either.

Although, *he* wasn't the one who might throw up the sandwich she'd eaten on the train any second now, because of a load of stupid hormones, so her sympathy only went so far.

'Do you believe me?' she asked quietly, when he still said nothing.

'Yes,' Cal replied. 'The lawyers will want the test, of course, but, yes. I believe you. I'm just trying to figure out what to do next.'

Heather gave him a small, lopsided smile. 'You and me both.'

He wasn't that much like Ross, now she'd got past the looks, Heather decided. Ross hadn't stopped talking the whole time they were together—about himself, about her, about places he'd been or wanted to go—yet he still hadn't managed to say any of the things that really mattered.

Cal, after his initial pitch for the nanny job, had been practically silent ever since she'd broken the news.

But he believed her. That was a big thing. She was clinging on to that.

'What did you hope to get from coming here today?' Cal asked finally.

Heather shrugged one shoulder. 'I'm not sure. Mostly I just wanted to tell Ross about the baby. I knew...' She swallowed. 'After I took the test, and he didn't answer his phone, I looked up the castle he'd talked about online. I saw the photos of him and his family on the website.

He didn't… When we met he wasn't wearing a wedding ring, and he didn't say anything to lead me to believe he was in a relationship, let alone married with kids.'

Cal's eyes fluttered shut for a second. 'No. I suppose he wouldn't have.'

'So I wasn't coming here for a happy-ever-after, or to demand that he marry me, or anything. I was sort of expecting him to throw me out, to be honest, so in some ways this is already going better than that.'

Apart from the bit where his brother was dead, of course. Oh, she was *really* screwing this up.

'Basically, I knew the right thing to do would be to tell Ross that he was going to be a father. Again. That's all I wanted. After that… Well, it would have been up to him. I just wanted to do the right thing.'

Because that mattered. She needed to be able to look her reflection in the eye when she caught sight of it in the mornings. She needed to know she'd done the right thing for her child.

The way her own mother hadn't.

And now she'd done that.

Which meant she had to figure out what the hell happened next on her own.

'The right thing?' Cal repeated the words with an ironic smile. As if there *was* such a thing in a woeful situation like this one.

He pitied that baby, being born into the Bryce family, with its legacy of screw-ups, scandals and sadness. What chance did it have?

Or perhaps he or she would be luckier than the rest of them. After all, this baby wouldn't have to grow up in Lengroth Castle, surrounded by reminders of the expectations the world placed upon it and knowing that if he or she didn't want to meet them, they'd have to learn how to hide the truth.

And, most of all, this baby would have Heather Reid, which was more than Ross's other two kids had. They were stuck with Uncle Cal, screwing them up for the rest of their childhoods.

Cal knew what Ross had been thinking when he'd named him as guardian—he'd been assuming it would never be needed. And who else was there, really? Who else would be able to understand the legacy of the Bryce family well enough to try and fix things for them all—or at least hide the truth a little longer?

Heather Reid wouldn't understand that, he'd bet. She was probably an honest, good girl, out of her depth in the pool of Lengroth scandals.

Of course, he could be overestimating her. Because, really, who travelled all the way from London to the wilds of Scotland just to 'do the right thing'? Nobody in Cal's family, that was for certain.

He wasn't sure any of his ancestors or relatives would even know what the right thing *was*, if it came calling. Not even Ross.

So, as trustworthy as Heather seemed, Cal knew better than to take those wide, innocent eyes at face value.

'Did you hope he'd support you financially?' he asked. That had to be it, right? Ross had told her he lived in a damn castle—of course she was after money. 'Or buy you off, so he didn't have to tell Janey?'

The worst part was that was probably exactly what Ross *would* have done. What Bryce men had been doing for generations to cover up their misdemeanours and betrayals. Hiding their scandals away under a blanket of hush money.

It was just that Cal had been so sure that Ross was different. And that if Ross could be different maybe he could, too. Maybe the scandal gene had skipped a generation, or something.

But here it was, fresh and revitalised for a whole new era of Bryces, ready to bring the Earldom of Lengroth into disrepute once and for all. Hiding bad behaviour had been a lot easier before the advent of social media.

Across the desk, he saw Heather's eyes had widened with shock. 'I didn't… *No.* Like I said—I have a job of my own. Supply teaching might not pay brilliantly, but I like working with the kids and it'll pay enough to support me *and* this baby, just. So, no, I wasn't expecting money. As I told you—if anything, I was expecting him to throw me out.'

'But you came anyway?'

'But I came anyway.'

Cal eyed her across the desk. She seemed genuine. Sincere. But then, people always did—until they screwed you over.

Then his gaze landed on the duck again. 'I have to ask...' He gestured towards it.

Spots of pink appeared on Heather's cheeks. 'Oh! It sort of...appeared in the moat as I was approaching the door. It seemed wrong to leave it there so I brought it in with me.'

Daisy, Cal was willing to bet. After tossing a bucket of water out of that nursery window a rubber duck was nothing. Practically a step down, in fact.

Cal thought wistfully of the time when he'd honestly believed that his niece and nephew were delightful, well-behaved children. When he'd lived thousands of miles away and only seen them for an afternoon at a time.

'How do you imagine the duck got there?' he asked Heather. 'In the moat, I mean?' An idea was starting to form somewhere in the back of his brain. It was entirely possible that it was a terrible idea, but it wasn't as if he had any better ones to go with. Especially since it seemed that the latest nanny from the agency hadn't even made it as far as the castle gates.

'Oh, I couldn't possibly say.'

There was a wry smile on Heather's face that

told Cal everything he needed to know. Firstly, that she knew *exactly* who must be responsible for the duck, but wasn't going to drop the kids in it. And, secondly, that Heather Reid was an open book, with her every thought and feeling shown on her face for him to read—as long as he could see it.

It was the second of those two facts that convinced him to follow the hare-brained plan that had evolved in his mind. After all, if he could see Heather's face he'd know when she was about to do something stupid. Like sell her story about her night with the Earl to the local papers. Or try to blackmail him for financial support. Or whatever.

And maybe, just maybe, what Daisy and Ryan really needed was someone on their side—the way Cal had always had Ross. And Cal had a feeling that Heather could be that person.

If she said yes.

Well, he'd never know if he didn't ask.

'So. You're pregnant with my niece or nephew. I am guardian to your baby's half-brother and half-sister. Clearly whatever happens next we're all in each other's lives now.'

Heather frowned. 'I… I suppose.'

Her lack of enthusiasm was, Cal supposed, understandable. He wouldn't want to be a part of this family either if he hadn't been born into it. Even then, actually. But he didn't have any choice. All he could do now was try and make growing up as a Bryce less awful for Daisy and Ryan than it had been for him and Ross. And he sure as hell couldn't do that on his own.

He took a breath and tried to smile as he said, 'In which case I have a proposition for you. If you'll hear it?'

He had no idea what to do next if she wouldn't.

A proposition? Heather remembered all too well what had happened *last* time a guy with the surname Bryce had propositioned her. But Cal didn't seem like the sort.

She'd come all this way. The least she could do was hear him out. After all, it wasn't as if she had any clear idea of her path forward. All she knew was that she needed to figure out a way to handle her situation without bringing scandal and shame down on her father. *Again.* He'd had enough of that for one lifetime, and last time… Well, the bottom line was she couldn't risk that happening again.

She needed to manage this carefully. Maybe Cal could help her do that.

'I'm listening,' she said neutrally, watching his expression.

Cal leaned forward in his chair, folded his hands on the desk next to the rubber duck and gazed straight into her eyes. 'I want you to stay here for the summer as nanny to Daisy and Ryan—Ross's children.'

Heather blinked. 'What?' She might have been less surprised if he'd suggested he ravish her over the desk, or that they set up a rubber duck factory together. 'I'm… I'm not a nanny.'

'No, you're a teacher. Which means you know kids a hell of a lot better than I do, for sure. Daisy and Ryan…they're ten and eight and they're struggling. They need someone who knows what they're doing and I think that person is you. Plus, teachers get great summer holidays, right?'

Six weeks. Six weeks in which she'd normally be planning for the next school year, sorting out her classroom, preparing supplies and resources… Except she'd been on a maternity leave cover contract for a year and, despite the promise of another position when the teacher she was covering for returned, last-minute budget cuts meant she didn't *actually* have a new job for September yet. No class to prepare for. And, given all the upheaval in her life, she'd figured some supply work might be best for the next term or so anyway. Until she figured out what she was doing.

All of which meant she really *didn't* have anything to do this summer.

She thought back to Cal's rambled job description when he'd thought she was Miss Thomas.

'If you stick out six weeks here at Castle Lengroth, and get the children prepared physically, mentally and emotionally for boarding school, I'll pay you for a full year's work at your agency base rate. But if you quit before the six weeks are up you get nothing.'

Did that offer still stand? A year's wages, even at nanny agency rates, would go an awful long way towards providing her with the cushion she needed to take care of this baby—and herself—until she got a new job. She could break the news of her pregnancy to her father in her own time and, while she'd have to tell *him* about the whole sleeping with a married earl thing, maybe no one else would need to know. It didn't seem that Cal was desperate to shout it from the rafters.

There'd be talk at home, of course. But an unmarried mother was a totally different thing to an aristocratic homewrecker. And very different again from last time, with her mother. Maybe it would be okay…

Besides, if things got bad she'd have money, and if she had money she had options. She could go and stay somewhere else for a while, until everything blew over. Take Dad with her, even. Maybe Wales, where they'd used to go on family holidays before.

Heather ran her tongue across her suddenly dry lips. 'What are the terms?'

She didn't *want* to spend the summer in Scotland. Not that she had anything against the country particularly, but it wasn't where she belonged. Especially not in this dark and foreboding castle with duck-wielding children.

But if *she* didn't want to be in this scary, imposing place, how must the kids feel about it? They'd grown up here, of course. But given what she knew of their father, and what she could therefore guess about their parents' marriage and family relationships, would that be a good thing or a bad thing?

'Same as if you really were the nanny from the agency,' Cal said. 'In fact, no one but us two need to know that you aren't. I think that would be better for now, don't you?'

Heather gave a slow nod. But *would* it be better? She wasn't good at secrets. She knew the harm they could do. But under the circumstances…what option did she have?

'So, you'd stay a full six weeks and get the children ready for boarding school—I have a folder with the details somewhere…' He looked around his immaculate desk, empty except for the rubber duck, then back at Heather. 'Or perhaps Mrs Peterson does. Anyway. You do that and I'll pay you a year's wages—not as a bribe, or because my brother got you into trouble, but because you'll have earned it.'

He'd anticipated her issues with the arrangement, Heather realised. As much as she could use the money, it *did* feel like a bribe—and that wasn't what she'd come here for. But he'd offered the money before he'd even known who she was, so it was a genuine payment for services rendered.

God, how bad *were* these kids?

At least there's only two of them. That can't be harder to handle than a class of thirty-four, right? And I manage them well enough.

Besides, teaching was one thing. Living with and supporting kids through important life changes was something else entirely. Something she needed to learn to do now she was going to become a mother.

'I don't suppose I can take some time to think about it?' she asked.

Cal shrugged. 'Honestly…? You might as well say yes now. Even if you leave in the next day or two nobody will be surprised. In fact, forty-eight hours will be more than the last nanny managed.'

'You're not selling this, you know.'

'I know.' Cal sighed. 'I'm not going to lie to you. The kids are hard work. I don't understand them, and I don't think they even *want* to be understood. Plus, the castle might actually be haunted—but you'll be long gone by Halloween, so hopefully that won't be an issue.'

'I don't believe in ghosts.' There were enough things in the real world to be terrified of, Heather had found, without adding a whole new fictional layer of fear.

'Even better.' Cal gave her a small smile—maybe the first she'd seen from him. It made him look younger, lighter. And even more handsome. 'The bottom line is, if you stay you can get to know your baby's family. And we can get to know you. You might decide you want nothing to do with us afterwards, but at least you'll have the information to make that decision with. And I'll get to help you financially without it being underhand or dodgy.'

'No one else will know why I'm really here?' Heather asked. That was important. 'I haven't… You're the only person who knows about the baby.'

He looked a little surprised at that. 'No one else will hear about it from me,' he promised.

And against her better judgement Heather believed him.

Six weeks. Six weeks to figure out what she wanted to do next and earn the money to pay for it. Six weeks to figure out how to admit to her father how badly she'd screwed up. To steel herself against his disappointment and upset.

Nannies were practically servants, right? And servants were prized for being invisible. Heather liked being invisible. If people didn't see you they were less likely to talk about you, taunt you or humiliate you.

She'd spent her childhood being part of the most talked about family in her small village. Here she could be completely anonymous— despite the scandal she carried inside her.

Six weeks.

How hard could that be?

She nodded. 'Okay.'

CHAPTER THREE

CAL HARDLY LET her get the word out before he pressed a button on the phone on his desk and called Mrs Peterson.

'Is she staying?' his housekeeper asked bluntly through the speakerphone. 'Or do I need to call another taxi? Only you know how much Harris hates driving all the way up here every time you lose another nanny. He'll be on his lunch break now, anyway.'

She made it sound as if he was misplacing them somewhere, in the nooks and crannies of the cavernous castle. As if they weren't actually running out through the front door without looking back.

The last one hadn't even waited for Harris—the driver of Lengroth village's only taxi—to show up. She'd walked the three miles to the station instead.

'Miss Reid is staying with us,' Cal said smugly.

'Reid?' He could almost hear Mrs Peterson's eyebrows rising. 'I thought the agency said her name was Thomas?'

Damn. He wasn't good at subterfuge. But he'd have to get better quickly if he was going to disguise his brother's pregnant mistress as a nanny for the next month and a half.

'A mix-up at the agency, it seems. Our new nanny is Miss Heather Reid.'

'I've stopped bothering to learn their names,' Mrs Peterson replied. 'Did the agency get the time of the interview wrong, too?'

'Yes. Yes, they did.' Mrs Peterson valued promptness highly, and what was one more little white lie if it smoothed the relationship between the nanny and the housekeeper of Lengroth Castle? 'In fact, Miss Reid was technically fifteen minutes early.'

'Hmph.'

Across the desk, Heather was looking most amused by his attempts to pacify his housekeeper. He resisted the urge to toss the rubber duck at her to stop her silent laughter.

'So if you could please come up to the office

and take Miss Reid for a tour of the castle, and to meet the children…?'

There was a loud sigh on the speakerphone. 'I suppose,' she said, and then the line went dead.

'Mrs Peterson is not a big fan of nannies?' Heather asked.

'To be honest, the last few we've had haven't really tried to endear themselves to her.' Cal tried to smile reassuringly. 'Mrs Peterson is a sweetheart when you get to know her, I promise.'

Heather looked sceptical.

But when Mrs Peterson arrived a few minutes later—Cal suspected she hadn't wasted time going all the way back down to the kitchen… she'd probably figured she'd be needed to show the nanny out before she even got that far—Heather smiled sweetly at her and talked about how excited she was to get to know the children and the castle.

'We'll see how long *that* lasts,' Mrs Peterson muttered ominously.

As they shut the door behind them Cal let out a long breath and sank down into his chair to process the last half an hour. Much as he'd far rather take a nap, there were still so many things to deal with.

So, taking stock…

Pluses: he had someone to look after Daisy and Ryan, hopefully for the rest of the summer, so he could get on with fixing everything their father, his brother, had screwed up before his death.

Minuses: that person was pregnant with Ross's child, and was basically another scandal waiting to happen.

Cal didn't think Heather was about to go running to the papers, seeking a pay-out for the headline *Adulterous Earl Fathers Baby from the Grave* or anything, but he knew better than most that appearances could be deceiving. At least this way he'd be keeping the scandal close to home, until he was sure of Heather's character. And the baby *was* a Bryce—he definitely believed that much.

Another nephew or niece for him to not know how to love. After all, it wasn't as if he'd ever been given any examples of loving parenthood, or even a loving relationship.

'Your heart's as cold as a Scottish winter,'

his latest ex-girlfriend had told him as she'd walked out. *'The view might be nice, but you wouldn't want to live there.'*

She might have had a point, he had to admit. But *his* life wasn't the problem here. Ross's was. And not just because of Heather.

With a sigh, Cal pulled over the folder sitting on the corner of his desk, sending the rubber duck toppling over as he did so. The folder's cover was blank—purposely. Cal didn't need a reminder to know what was inside it.

Another of his big brother's follies.

Living the lives they did, the Earls of Lengroth had never been particularly good at holding on to their money. Fortunately the estate was still reasonably lucrative—with most of it rented out to farmers or tenants in the linked village. But the castle took a lot of upkeep, which required all that money.

At least it did when there was someone sensible at the reins—usually an estate manager or the current Countess of Lengroth.

Ross, however, seemed to have believed he could do it all himself. Or maybe he'd felt he *needed* to, in order to keep his secrets. Because what Ross mostly seemed to have done with the estate finances was gamble it away.

Cal's eyes fluttered closed as he tried, for an unsavoury moment, to imagine his perfect big brother at the gambling tables, throwing away his children's inheritance. Or in a London bar, seducing Heather Reid.

The latter was alarmingly easy. With that river of copper hair, and those soft green eyes, Cal could easily imagine any man's attention being drawn to her, even across a darkened bar.

He opened his eyes again. *Not helping, Cal.* Especially since he liked to think—in his better moments—that he might actually be able to resist the kind of scandalous fall from grace that seemed to afflict all the Earls of Lengroth sooner or later.

'But I'm *not* the Earl,' he muttered to himself.

He was going to do everything in his power to stop Ryan from following that same path. But first he had to finish fixing Ross's mistakes.

He flipped open the folder, ready to start again.

Most of the basic gambling debts he'd dealt

with up front, the moment he'd found them. He should have used the estate money, he knew, but that was Ryan's, and Cal didn't want his nephew to be saddled with money troubles from the outset. Fortunately Cal's own property business in the States was lucrative enough that he'd had enough personal wealth to fill the hole. His accountant hadn't been happy about it, but then neither was Cal, really.

More problematic to deal with were the times when Ross had clearly tried to use his title and minor celebrity in place of money. Or to impress, Cal supposed. He wasn't sure what else would explain the obligation sitting on top of the pile, waiting for him to fix it. An email from a magazine editor, confirming plans made with Ross for later in the summer.

'Why on earth would Ross have invited a reporter to come and stay at the castle?' he wondered aloud, rubbing a hand over his eyes as if that would change the contents of the printout in front of him.

It didn't.

Only one way to find out, Cal supposed.

He picked up the phone to try and explain to

this editor that, with Ross dead, there was no way in hell he was letting a journalist anywhere near Lengroth Castle this summer.

She'd left the rubber duck in Cal's office, Heather realised as Mrs Peterson showed her yet another identical green and grey room in the cold, dead castle. She should have brought it with her—either as a peace offering or a sign that she couldn't be intimidated by flying bath toys.

Except she was, of course—intimidated. And not just by ducks.

Thirty-four children in a classroom were one thing. Two children alone in a castle, with a ghost and a revolving door for nannies, were something completely different.

Heather felt sick again. Didn't this castle have *any* bathrooms? She wasn't sure that Mrs Peterson had shown her one.

'And this will be your room,' Mrs Peterson said finally, opening the door on a grey room with a grey metal bed and a green and grey tartan bedspread. There was a chair by the window, looking out over the front of the castle all the way to the grey gates. Heather wondered if this was where Daisy had thrown the duck from.

'Is there a bathroom?' Heather entered the room cautiously, looking for a bathroom door and possibly a ghost, or a child waiting to jump out at her and pelt her with bath toys. She saw neither.

'Down the hall,' Mrs Peterson answered. 'Lengroth Castle was built before the advent of your modern en suite bathrooms, you realise.'

Lengroth Castle had clearly been built before indoor plumbing, central heating, electricity and Wi-Fi technology, too, but Heather sincerely hoped *they'd* all been included in any subsequent remodelling.

'Down the hall? Right...'

Feeling she'd taken in enough of the room, Heather dumped her rucksack beside the bed, turned to Mrs Peterson and said, 'So, shall we go and meet the children?' in her best Mary Poppins voice.

Mrs Peterson looked suspicious.

'I mean, that *is* what I'm here for,' Heather went on, knowing she was babbling and unable to stop herself. 'To be a nanny, I mean.' And definitely not the bearer of the children's illegitimate half-sibling or anything. *No, sir.*

Oh, she was *terrible* at lying. Clearly she took after her father and not her mother there. Why had she ever thought she could pull this off?

But after a long moment Mrs Peterson stepped back, out of the doorway. 'The nursery is this way.'

She click-clacked off down the corridor, her heels echoing off the stone walls, and stopped at the next door, a good ten metres away.

Heather steeled herself, and followed.

'Children,' Mrs Peterson said as she opened the nursery door, 'this is Miss Reid, your new nanny.' She sounded almost…*fond*, Heather realised. Which, given what she knew of the children so far, didn't make much sense.

Unless they were in it together, determined to drive away any newcomers to the castle.

Heather was so engaged in a sudden daydream of Mrs Peterson dressing up in a white sheet pretending to be a ghost, while Daisy and Ryan stood behind her hurling rubber ducks at an invading army of nannies, that she almost forgot to greet the children.

'Hello! You can call me Heather. And you two must be Daisy and Ryan!' She was still channelling Mary Poppins, she realised. If she wasn't careful she might burst into song at any moment.

'She doesn't look like the other nannies,' Ryan said, eyeing her with suspicion.

His dark hair was curled over his forehead, so like his father's and his uncle's that Heather felt a pang of sympathy all over again.

Mrs Peterson looked at Heather and sighed. 'No. No, she doesn't.'

'Maybe that means I'll last longer than they did,' Heather replied, a little archly.

Mrs Peterson's mouth flickered into something that might almost, *almost* be considered a smile. If she squinted. The almost smile was gone so quickly that Heather wasn't entirely sure she hadn't imagined it.

'Daisy. Come and say hello to Miss Reid.'

Over at the window, looking out over the very steps Heather had climbed to get into the castle, sat Daisy. She must take after her mother,

Heather decided, given the pale mousy hair, braided into thin plaits that hung over her thinner shoulders. There was nothing about Daisy that spoke of the broad-shouldered confidence the Bryce men seemed to be born with.

Then she turned away from the window to face Heather and pierced her with sharp, intelligent amber eyes that were all her Uncle Cal.

'Nannies don't wear baggy jumpers,' she said, looking Heather up and down. 'Or trainers.'

'Well, this one does,' Heather said cheerfully.

These kids had better get used to her wardrobe, since she hadn't brought anything smart in her small rucksack. In fact, she hadn't brought much of anything. A single change of clothing, her phone charger, that sort of thing. She hadn't been planning on staying, after all. She'd have to find out if Cal's generous employment deal included an advance for suitable work wear.

'I'll leave you to it, then, Miss Reid,' Mrs Peterson said, as if she were saying, *I hope the lions don't eat you, but they probably will.*

'Heather, please,' she tried one last time, but Mrs Peterson ignored her.

'Dinner is at six in the dining hall,' she added, closing the door behind her.

Heather looked at the children. The children looked at Heather, clearly waiting for her to break first.

They'd broken eight different nannies, Heather remembered uncomfortably. But they wouldn't break her. Because Heather knew something that they didn't.

They were family. Or they would be once this baby was born. And if Heather had learned one thing from her taunting, scandal-ridden childhood, it was this: you never ran out on family.

'Right,' she said, clapping her hands together *à la* Mary Poppins. 'Mrs Peterson has shown me all around the inside of the castle—how about you two show me around outside?'

Daisy and Ryan exchanged a look that Heather couldn't read.

'Outside?' Daisy asked suspiciously, as if there had to be a catch somewhere.

'Yep. I saw some great-looking woodland on my way in—I bet that's fun to explore.' She shot a sideways look at Daisy, who was trying to communicate something to her brother using only her eyebrows. 'Plus, I understand that the castle moat has some very unusual ducks in it.'

Ryan stifled a snigger at that, while Daisy glared at him so hard that Heather thought lasers might shoot out of her eyes.

'Come on! It's summer. You two should be outside, enjoying the glorious sunshine.' Heather glanced out of the window. 'But grab your wellies on the way, yeah?'

They *were* in Scotland, after all.

The dining hall at Lengroth Castle was large, cold, prone to damp and currently mostly empty.

From the head of the oversized table Cal stared down at the vacant seats arranged around him. Alone, it was almost too easy for him to remember them occupied by Ross, or their parents. Even society's brightest and best, in the castle's heyday, before his father's rages had taken greater hold and entertaining had become just too risky.

Right now, though, all that was missing was his niece, his nephew and his new nanny.

'Dinner will be cold,' Mrs Peterson said, speaking volumes with her tone.

With just those four innocent words, Cal knew exactly what she was *really* asking.

Who is this Miss Reid? Why is she here? Do you really *expect me to believe that the local agency sent her, with an accent like that?* And, most importantly, *What has she done with the children?*

'I'm sure they'll be here soon,' Cal said, as mildly as he could. 'Miss Reid seems like a very responsible person.' Apart from sleeping with strange, married earls she met in London bars. 'And her references are impeccable.'

She was practically family, after all. And if Cal's parents had taught him anything about family it was that they knew where the bodies were buried, so you had to keep them close.

'Hmm...' Mrs Peterson said, speaking volumes once more with just one noise.

Suddenly the huge, wooden door of the castle crashed open.

'Sorry we're late!'

Heather's English tones rang through the castle corridors, probably reaching them a good thirty seconds after she spoke, due to the distance from the door to the dining room. Clearly she had some lungs on her.

'Where's the damn...? I mean, Daisy, where's the dining room?'

The last was quieter, but sound carried well in the castle. Something Cal had had reason to curse plenty of times in his life.

'I think they're here,' Cal said redundantly, and Mrs Peterson gave him a look that suggested that, given their joint ability to state the obvious, he and Miss Reid deserved each other.

'I'm so sorry!' Heather gasped as she and the children barrelled through the big double doors at one end of the dining hall. Not the end nearest to the front door, Cal noticed, which meant that Ryan had been playing his usual trick of trying to get the new nanny disorientated and lost.

He blinked as he took in the full impact of their appearance. Behind him Mrs Peterson made a faint noise of either astonishment, disgust, or both.

Mud was dripping from Heather's nose. And her hair. And her sodden jumper. The skirt of her sundress was caked in mud, and there were twigs in her cascading copper hair.

Daisy and Ryan were suspiciously clean by comparison.

Cal surveyed his niece and nephew, both of whom appeared to be working hard at maintaining an air of innocence. Then he met Heather's gaze and saw there a determination and steeliness that surprised him with its depth.

It's going to take more than a fall in the river to scare this one off, kids.

At least, that was what he assumed had happened. It was what they'd done to nanny number three, anyway. There was a stretch where the bridge didn't *quite* reach the far bank—not since the river had swelled and burst its banks the winter before. It was simple enough to jump to safety via the stepping stones on the other side, but only if you knew to look for them. If you weren't paying proper attention when you reached the end of the bridge—say if an evil child was distracting you by dangling from a tree, or something—it was easy to miss the fact that the bridge basically gave way to a river of mud.

'Miss Reid, perhaps you would like to freshen up before dinner?' Mrs Peterson said, as if Heather had merely a smudge of dust on her nose or something.

Ryan snorted. Daisy, as ever, remained implacable. The girl was definitely her mother's daughter, Cal decided. Janey must have known what Ross was really like—what was going on behind her back. But he'd never seen a glimpse of it in her calm, serene expression.

Heather gave a grateful smile. 'I won't be long. Children, why don't you come with me? We can all change for dinner.'

'But *we're* not muddy,' Ryan protested.

They hadn't eaten since lunch, what with the impromptu nature ramble Heather had taken them on, so Cal assumed the boy must be starving. He knew *he* was.

'The great outdoors is full of all sorts of germs, though,' Heather said airily. 'You definitely need to wash before you eat. Maybe even have a bath…'

There was a wicked twinkle in her eye. One Cal approved of mightily.

'But our dinner will get cold,' Daisy said, perfectly reasonably.

Heather pulled an expression of regretful sorrow Cal was *almost* sure was fake.

'I know—I'm *so* sorry. So *clumsy* of me to slip in the mud on the bridge. If only I'd known that the bridge ended short of the riverbank I wouldn't have spent so long flailing around in the mud, waiting for you two to come down from the trees and help me up. And then we wouldn't have been late for dinner.'

She flashed a quick smile at Cal and Mrs Peterson.

'All my fault, you see. But the children and I really *must* clean ourselves up before dinner. Please, don't wait for us, though.'

She ushered the children out of the dining room, Ryan still grumbling as they went. Cal watched them go, smiling. This might all work out a lot better than even he had planned.

'I make that one to Miss Reid and nil to Daisy and Ryan,' Mrs Peterson murmured softly.

Cal glanced up to see that the older woman had a small smile on her face. One he didn't think he'd seen since he'd returned for Ross's funeral.

'I think you're right,' he replied. 'Now, do you think we can reheat dinner?'

CHAPTER FOUR

THE ENFORCED PRE-DINNER baths hadn't made
Heather any more popular with the children—
or with Cal and Mrs Peterson, she imagined,
since they'd both waited to eat with them. But
then falling in a muddy riverbank hadn't really
endeared Daisy, Ryan or Lengroth Castle itself
to Heather, so she didn't feel too bad about it.

If nothing else, she'd shown the children that
their actions had consequences.

It seemed to be working—for now, anyway.
And by the time Heather was showered and
changed—and thank heaven for whoever had
upgraded the castle plumbing, even if they
hadn't given her an en suite bathroom—the
children were also scrubbed and dressed.

'Great!' she said, eyeing the bathroom that
linked the children's bedrooms—which she
was almost certain classified as en suite, whatever Mrs Peterson said. 'Now, if you just pick

up those wet towels and put your dirty clothes in the washing basket we can all get some dinner.'

Her stomach rumbled and she hoped the kids didn't hear it. Hunger was a sign of weakness. She couldn't afford to show any more weakness in front of them now they'd seen her flailing around in the mud, helpless.

There were mutters and glares, but the towels were picked up. Heather held in a smile. They were getting somewhere.

Back down in the dining room Heather had expected to find Cal gone, sure that he'd have already eaten. But instead he and Mrs Peterson were waiting for them, and as they appeared in the doorway, pink from scrubbing, hair sleek and still wet, she disappeared to the kitchen to get the food.

Cal raised an eyebrow at her and Heather was suddenly very aware that she probably didn't look much older than Daisy, with her copper hair in two heavy, wet plaits that hung over her shoulders. There hadn't been time to dry it, even though the castle still held a chill, despite it being the middle of summer.

She slipped into the chair at the place setting furthest away from him, and watched to make sure that the children took their seats nicely, too.

Perhaps they were worn out from fighting her all afternoon, because they sat down without any fuss at all. Or perhaps they were just saving their energy for a renewed resistance tomorrow.

Mrs Peterson returned with hot plates and a dinner of pie and vegetables, which Heather devoured happily. Across the table she could see Daisy passing Ryan her meat and taking his vegetables in return, but since they both ate plenty she decided to pick her battles.

They ate mostly in silence. Heather had many questions she wanted to ask, but not in front of the children. Besides, she got the impression that Mrs Peterson would be scandalised by most of the things she wanted to know.

She wanted to know more about the father of her child. Was that so unusual?

There was pudding after the pie—some sort of sloppy custard thing that the children and Cal ate happily but that renewed Heather's pregnancy sickness with a vengeance. She pushed the bowl away and hoped she didn't look too green. Mrs Peterson pulled an offended face, but Heather was pretty sure she'd have been more offended if she'd eaten it and then thrown it up again.

God, she was tired. This day had already been so much longer than she'd anticipated, and she'd barely had any time alone to process the events of it. It didn't look as if she was going to get any time to herself just yet, either. After all, there was still bedtime to get through, and she couldn't see Daisy and Ryan going quietly to sleep.

Cal was watching her, she realised as she looked up from the bowl of pudding. No, not watching. *Studying.* She tried to sit up straighter, and even contemplated taking an actual mouthful of dessert until a strong wave of nausea told her not even to think about it.

'Mrs Peterson,' Cal said suddenly. 'As Miss Reid has already bathed and changed the children into their pyjamas, perhaps you could supervise bedtime tonight? I have some contract issues to discuss with Miss Reid.'

Heather shot him a grateful smile as Mrs Peterson agreed and ushered the children out of the dining room, making them pause in the doorway to say a dutiful but insincere goodnight.

And then it was just the two of them.

'You look dead on your feet,' Cal said.

Heather didn't bother to deny it.

'Come on. We'll go through to my sitting room. I need a brandy. And you can have… something else,' he said, vaguely, obviously remembering that alcohol was not on the menu for her for the next seven months. Longer, if she breastfed.

In fact, given what had happened the last time she'd drunk alcohol, Heather rather thought she might give it up all together. Just to be on the safe side.

Cal's sitting room was warm, cosy and welcoming in a way that nowhere else in the castle Heather had seen so far had managed. She curled up in the armchair near the unlit fireplace, and pulled a blanket over her knees more for comfort than warmth.

Cal handed her a glass of something frosty and misty before pouring himself a brandy.

Heather cautiously took a sip. It was delicious.

'Home-made elderflower cordial and sparkling water,' Cal said, taking his own seat opposite her. 'Mrs Peterson makes it.'

'It's lovely.' Heather took another sip.

'Better with champagne,' Cal replied. 'But under the circumstances... Speaking of which—what happened by the river? You didn't hurt yourself or the baby? I should have asked before... Do you want me to take you to the hospital to get checked? I'll be honest, I don't really know how these things work.'

Heather smiled at his concern. 'Neither do I, really. But I didn't fall hard or anything. Just slipped into the mud at the end of the bridge. More embarrassing than painful—which I imagine was just what the children intended.'

'Probably,' Cal admitted. 'So you don't need the hospital?'

Heather shook her head. 'I'm fine.' Then a thought occurred to her and she frowned. 'But I do need to transfer my medical care up here if I'm staying. To keep up my midwife appointments and scans and what have you.' She hadn't even thought about that side of things when she'd agreed to Cal's deal.

'And are you?' he asked, pausing with his glass halfway to his lips as he waited for her answer.

Heather frowned. 'Am I what?'

'Staying.'

Cal had no idea what he was going to do if she said no now. Of course she'd been happy to take his deal before she'd met the kids. But an afternoon with Daisy and Ryan—not to mention Mrs Peterson's disapproving gaze—might well have changed her mind.

But if she could put up with a mud dunking from his niece and nephew, maybe she'd be strong enough to stick it out. To be honest, she already seemed to have more control over them after one afternoon than some of the previous nannies had had after a week or more.

Heather was the right person for this job— Cal could feel it. And not just because she was a scandalous time bomb waiting to explode.

She still hadn't answered. That was a bad sign, right? Or maybe she was just making very sure of her answer. She didn't seem like the impulsive type—her encounter with Ross notwithstanding.

Finally she nodded, and Cal let out the breath he'd been holding and took a celebratory sip of his brandy.

'I'm staying,' Heather confirmed. 'Which means there's a lot of things we need to sort out.'

'I can give you the details of our family doctor. He's been looking after the Bryces for decades.' *And keeping their secrets.* 'He'll look after you. It's only for six weeks, after all.'

How many appointments would she need in that time anyway?

'I suppose… But my twelve-week scan is due soon. I'll need to get that moved to the nearest hospital with a maternity unit. Which is…?'

'Edinburgh, I imagine,' Cal replied, thankful possibly for the first time for the remote location and lack of facilities at Lengroth. At least in Edinburgh he was unlikely to be recognised and asked a lot of awkward questions. 'We'll get Dr Harvey to book it for you, and I'll take you down to the city for it.'

She looked surprised at his offer. 'Thank you.'

Cal shifted uncomfortably under her grateful gaze. 'Of course. It's only right. Now, what else do you need now you're staying?'

'Clothes,' Heather said, pulling a face. 'Probably maternity ones before too long, I suppose. Um…teaching materials for the children? Do they have laptops? I didn't bring mine, and it would be good to get them to do some online tests and figure out where they're at with their learning.'

'Can online quizzes test cunning and guile?' Cal asked. 'Because they'd probably ace those.'

Heather shook her head, a small smile on her face. 'I get the feeling that they're so used to acting up to get attention from people they've forgotten how to be any other way.'

'And you're going to remind them?' Cal asked.

Heather nodded. 'Well, me *and* you.'
Wait. What?
Cal put down his glass and frowned at her.

'You *do* remember our deal here, Miss Reid, right?'

Heather rolled her eyes. 'You really don't have to call me that, you know. Especially when Mrs Peterson isn't listening.'

'Fine. Heather, then. Our deal…?'

'I spend the next six weeks getting the children ready for whichever awful boarding school you're shipping them off to, and you pay me lots of money and give me whatever I need to make it happen.'

'I think you added the last bit yourself, but fine.' Cal shook his head as her other words caught up with him. 'And the school isn't awful. In fact, Derryford Academy is one of the most highly regarded boarding schools in the country. Ross and I both went there.'

Heather muttered something that sounded suspiciously like, *Explains a lot…* under her breath. Cal ignored her.

'And the fact it's such a good school is why I need you here—to make sure their academics are up to scratch. They're coming in late as it is. Ross wanted to send them as soon as they were old enough, but Janey insisted on keeping them at home, so...' He shrugged.

There was a peculiar look on Heather's face. It took Cal a moment to realise what it was. Pain.

'Were you in love with my brother?' he asked softly.

If she had been... Well, he could only imagine how painful this whole situation was for her. She'd claimed it was only a one-night stand, but people lied—he knew that well enough. And maybe she hadn't wanted to admit to him, Ross's brother, about a long-term affair.

Heather shot him a surprised look. 'No! I told you, it was just one night. I barely even knew him.'

She sounded convincing, but liars often did. 'You looked in actual agony when I mentioned his wife,' he pointed out.

Another flash of pain spread across her face, contradicting her words. Cal was just starting to feel smug about his ability to see through her lies when she spoke again.

'I wasn't in love with Ross, Cal. I barely knew him. In fact, if I *had* known him I never would have gone back to his hotel room with him that night. If I'd known he was married...that he had children...'

She shuddered, and Cal realised he'd read her all wrong after all. He kept doing that with this woman. Normally he prided himself on being able to see through the lies and the covers people put up to mask their real feelings and actions. What made Heather so different?

Then he realised.

She wasn't lying to him.

'If I feel pain, it's for his wife. For his kids. For the mistakes I made,' Heather went on. 'I should have asked more questions, been more certain, before I went back with him. That's a mistake that's going to haunt me for a long time.'

'Because of the baby?' Cal guessed.

He *wanted* to understand her, he realised. To figure out how she could be so open and honest about her feelings and actions when it seemed like no one else he'd ever known could.

Heather shook her head and a bright smile spread across her face, transforming the atmosphere in the room. 'This baby is the best thing to come from that night. And, however many mistakes *I* made to get to this point, I know that a baby is never a mistake. He or she is a new life, a new chance for happiness—for them, and maybe even for me.'

Cal sat back in his chair, amazed. 'You're really not like other people, are you?'

Heather pulled a face. 'I don't know what you mean.'

And she didn't, he realised. Because this was just who she was—open and honest and without guile or lies. No wonder he hadn't got a clue what to make of her.

'It doesn't matter,' he said, shaking his head. 'What matters is that you're staying and that you'll get the kids ready for school in time.'

He needed to focus on the important stuff, the big picture—not get carried away trying to make sense of his brother's one-night stand. Like getting the kids out of the castle. And keeping that damn reporter from *Elite* magazine away from Lengroth altogether.

His conversation with the editor had not been encouraging; apparently she was sending over a copy of the contract for Cal's lawyers to look at. And she'd made it very clear that he did *not* want to be found in breach of it…

He shook away that concern for another time and turned his attention back to Heather. But she just added another layer to the issue. The last thing he needed was a reporter staying at the castle alongside the woman who was carrying the late Earl's illegitimate child.

'Are you okay?' Heather asked, with genuine concern in her voice. 'You're kind of…staring.'

He looked away. Quickly. 'Sorry. Just…lots on my mind. Picking up all the loose threads after Ross… You know…'

'Of course.' Heather got quickly and neatly to her feet. 'I'll leave you to it. I need to get to bed if I'm going to start teaching the children tomorrow.'

She smoothed down the sundress she was wearing under a chunky knitted cardigan. She wasn't showing at all yet, Cal realised. Would she be by the end of the summer? He didn't know. If she was nearly twelve weeks, as she said, then she'd be four and half months by September.

Halfway through, he thought. Hopefully by

then he'd have some idea of what to do about her and the baby. But for now…

'I'll arrange for laptops for all three of you. And I'll get a credit card for you, linked to the castle account. You'll be able to order whatever clothes you need, teaching supplies…that sort of thing.'

'Thank you.' Heather's wide smile was grateful. 'That would be wonderful.'

He'd set a generous limit on the card, Cal decided as she left the room. See how close she came to reaching it. If she did—well, who *wouldn't* make the most of that opportunity? And if she didn't…maybe she really was different from the other people in his life.

Either way, the children would be out of his hair and someone else's problem. That was what really mattered.

Heather was awoken early the next morning, before the sun had even crept over the hills, by the sound of shrieking. High-pitched, ear-ringing, brain-hurting, shrieking.

She blinked, trying to remember where

she was, what was happening, who could be screaming…

Daisy.

Throwing the covers aside, she raced to the doorway that led to the hall, then down the short distance to the children's rooms.

The stone floors of the castle were freezing under her bare feet, even in summer. Heather didn't care. She burst into Daisy's room and found Ryan already there, huddled in a heap at the end of her bed, his hands over his ears.

'Daisy. *Daisy.*'

It wasn't good to wake a dreamer. Or was that a sleepwalker? Either way, Heather knew she had to do it. She gave the girl a small shake on her shoulder. Then a harder one.

Daisy's eyes popped open. 'You shouldn't be in my room after lights out,' she said, for all the world as if she'd just awoken from a restful nap.

Heather shared a quick glance with Ryan, who just shrugged. 'She always does this.'

Does what? Heather wondered. Scream, dream or pretend it never happened?

'You were screaming,' Heather said soothingly. 'Did you have a bad dream?'

'No,' Daisy said sharply, but Heather would have known it was a lie even without the shrieking. Her eyes were wide and terrified, red and raw around the edges.

'Do you want to talk about it?' Heather asked.

Daisy rolled over to face the wall, pulled the blanket up to her chin and stubbornly shut her eyes. 'I want to go back to sleep. Alone.'

Heather waited a few minutes, but Daisy showed no signs of moving or talking. Her breathing was too shallow for her to be asleep, but Heather knew she was stubborn enough to pretend all the way until morning.

Time to try a different approach.

Getting quietly to her feet, as if she really did believe Daisy was sleeping and didn't want to wake her, Heather motioned to Ryan to follow her back through the linked bathroom to his room. Once the connecting doors were closed behind them, Heather smiled and spoke at a more normal volume.

'Come on, let's get you tucked in again, too.'

It was the first time she'd been alone with Ryan, she realised—without Daisy's glares and nudges to control his reactions. She planned to take advantage of it.

'Does she often have nightmares?' Heather asked as she shook out his duvet.

Ryan nodded sleepily. 'Most nights. But she doesn't always scream. Sometimes she just whimpers, and then she calms down again when I go in and lie down with her.'

These poor children. Stuck in this castle, grieving for their parents, and now their uncle wants to send them away to boarding school.

Cal was concerned that their academic learning should be up to the standard required at Derryford Academy. Heather was far more worried about ensuring that their mental and emotional well-being was up to living there.

And right now she wasn't at all sure it was.

'Do you have nightmares, too?' Heather asked softly.

Ryan's eyes were already drifting closed again, proving more than his words that this really was an everyday occurrence for him.

'Sometimes,' he murmured, his voice heavy with sleep. 'But not like Daisy.'

His breathing evened out and Heather knew

he was asleep again. She'd have to save her questions for another time.

In the meantime... *I need to do more reading. Learn about grieving children...how to help them.*

But one thing she already knew. Whatever these children had been through, they needed the same thing all children needed. Love, understanding and someone to listen. They needed to feel secure and safe.

And, judging by Daisy's nightmares—not to mention the mud incident and the flying rubber duck—they didn't.

Heather knew what it was like to grow up without one parent. She couldn't imagine how she'd have coped if she'd lost her father as well as her mother. But she could identify a little with Daisy and Ryan.

The children were playing defence—attacking anyone who came near before they could *be* attacked. Heather wasn't sure what form they expected that attack to come in, but they were definitely expecting it.

She needed to find a way to show them that they were safe and loved. But she was only staying until September. She wasn't a long-term solution here.

But she knew a man who was.

These children needed family. And right now that family consisted of their uncle Cal—a man who planned to ship them off to boarding school so he didn't have to deal with them.

Not if she could help it.

Tucking Ryan in one last time, she left the children sleeping to head back to her own room, already planning how best to approach Cal with her ideas.

She shut the bedroom door quietly, turned— and screamed.

CHAPTER FIVE

CAL CLAPPED A hand over Heather's mouth to stop her screaming. The last thing they needed after all this was Daisy waking up and starting to shriek again. There was only so much night-time noise his ears could take.

'It's me. Cal. Not a ghost, or whatever.'

He'd never even seen a hint of the damn thing, but every other nanny seemed convinced that the castle was haunted, so why would Heather be any different. *Of course* she'd screamed.

He'd automatically pulled her into his arms, he realised belatedly, and the soft curves under her pyjamas were pressed up against his bare chest and boxers. *Not* the most professional start to their working relationship. But, God, it felt good.

The strange feeling that had made him stare at her earlier that evening swept over him again—half-amazement, half-disbelief that she was even real.

One thing was definitely real, though, and that was the way she felt in his arms. If this were any other woman he'd definitely be thinking about kissing her right now. About keeping her this close the whole night long...

Except she was his employee, *and* she was carrying his brother's child, so this was the most inappropriate line of thought ever.

Oh, who was he kidding? He was thinking it anyway.

'I'm not screaming any more,' Heather said, sounding far more calm and rational than he felt, with her copper curls tickling his neck and the scent of her filling his lungs.

Cal let go. Quickly.

'Sorry,' he said, stepping away. 'I just didn't want you to wake the kids again.'

'I kind of got that.'

Why was she looking at him that way? She couldn't *know* all the things he'd been thinking about doing to her as her body touched his, right? At least she'd brought him to his senses before his lower body had *really* started to react to the situation.

Cal thought many calming thoughts and hoped the corridor was dark enough to hide his blushes. And other things.

'So…uh… Daisy had another nightmare?' he asked redundantly.

Heather nodded. 'Ryan says she has them a lot. Sorry, I probably should have waited for you to go in—'

'No!' Cal said, sharply. 'No. You're the nanny— it's your place.'

Her expression turned curious, and then disapproving in turn, with the pale, wan light from the lamp on the wall highlighting the planes and shadows of her face.

'You're their uncle,' she said. 'It's more your place than mine.'

Cal shook his head. 'I tried once. She threw pillows at me and screeched even louder than she did when she was dreaming. Trust me, it's better for everyone that you do it.'

Heather was still staring at him. Assessing him. He didn't like it. Even if her scrutiny had finally got his body back on board with their strictly professional relationship terms.

'You want the children to be ready to go to boarding school in six weeks?' she said slowly, as if she were just catching up to how difficult that would be.

'That's the idea.'

'Then you're going to have to show them that it's safe for them to leave. And come back again.'

Cal frowned. 'Is this something to do with the ghost? Have you been having some sort of séance when I wasn't looking?'

Maybe he should get an exorcist in, or something. Did they come for atheists? He wasn't sure.

'It's not the damn ghost they're afraid of,' Heather snapped. 'I told you—I don't even believe in them.'

'Then what is it?'

Heather's smile was small and sad. 'Everything else.'

'That makes no sense. They're rich, privileged kids.' Or they would be, once Cal had sorted out the castle's precarious financial situation. 'What do they have to be scared of?'

'They've lost their *parents*, Cal,' Heather snapped, clearly at the end of her patience with his lack of understanding. 'Their whole world has shifted, and nothing they placed their trust in before has held true. They don't know what or who to believe in, and they don't know what's going to happen next. Of course they're terrified.'

'Well, when you put it like that...' Cal rubbed the back of his neck tiredly, wishing he could go back to bed. No, wishing he could go back in time to when none of this had been his problem. When Ross had still been the perfect older brother who could be relied on to take care of all the family stuff.

But that had all been lies anyway.

'Did you honestly not think about how their parents' deaths must have affected them?' Heather asked, more softly now.

'No, I did. I just...'

How could he explain that when his own parents had died he'd felt nothing. That, growing up, he'd sometimes daydreamed about what would happen if his father *did* die. Would their mother suddenly realise she loved them after all? Realise that they were more than just an heir and a spare?

Even in his daydreams he hadn't really believed it.

But Ross and Janey had been different—or so he'd believed. He'd hoped they really *did* love their children, the way he and Ross had always wanted to be loved.

Now, with everything he'd learned about Ross and his marriage since their death, Cal realised he'd begun to see them as just like his parents.

'Of course I did. I knew they were grieving, that they missed them. But by the time I arrived here and took over, on the day of the funeral, they were both already so cold. Distant. I just assumed...'

First he'd assumed that they knew he couldn't give them what they needed. That he was no good at this family stuff and had no idea how to be a guardian. Then, later, he'd assumed they felt the same way about Ross and Janey as he had about his own parents' deaths.

But he had a feeling Heather wouldn't understand any of that.

'My first priority was to get the estate management and its finances under control,' he said instead. 'Ross… It turned out things weren't in as great a shape as I'd been led to believe. This is the kids' future security and livelihood. I was looking out for their futures.'

'They need security *now*, Cal. And not the financial type. They need love.'

Then they were out of luck. Because love was one thing Cal had no experience or knowledge of.

'Then love them,' he said, turning on his heel to head back to his cold, lonely bedroom.

Heather would have to learn to love them as their half-sibling's mother.

Because he knew that *he* couldn't.

Heather's eyes were gritty with sleep when she awoke late the next morning. After the pre-dawn antics with Daisy, and that disturbing conversation with Cal, it had taken her an age to get back to sleep again. And when she finally had her dreams had been restless—filled with a strange sense of longing, desperation and the remembrance of a body against hers. She'd assumed it to be Ross—until her eyes had flashed open and she'd realised it was Cal.

Added to her general pregnancy tiredness, the disturbed night meant that she was totally exhausted. And she still had to go into battle today—with and for Daisy and Ryan.

She showered quickly in the chilly bathroom down the corridor, then dressed in the same sundress and cardigan she'd worn for dinner. Until Cal came good on his clothes-shopping promise her wardrobe was severely limited. Thank goodness she always packed extra underwear in case of emergency.

Being properly prepared was important. Which was why she practised all her arguments and approaches towards Cal as she got ready to face the day.

The periodic nausea that had plagued her for weeks seemed to be abating at last, which was something. In every other way she felt totally unprepared for the day ahead.

She was missing something about Cal, she decided as she brushed her teeth, grateful that the toothpaste didn't make her gag for the first time in weeks. He seemed like a good guy, genuinely trying to help his niece and nephew—but in all the wrong ways. Could she show him the right ones in the next six weeks?

She hoped so.

'Ah, Miss Reid. So good of you to join us.'

Mrs Peterson nodded pointedly to the table, already laid with breakfast, as Heather entered the dining room. Daisy and Ryan were in their seats, and Cal was reading a newspaper on his tablet at the head of the table. A slight heat rose to Heather's cheeks as she remembered him as she'd seen him last—half-naked in the dark, his arms around her waist.

Damn her pregnancy hormones. They'd had her body in a spin just at the closeness of him—at least as soon as her initial terror had worn off and she'd realised who it was that held her.

Not that the 'who' made it any better. Next to Ross Bryce, the second most inappropriate person for her to be fantasising about had to be his brother.

With an apologetic smile Heather slipped into

her seat as the others started to help themselves to toast, eggs, fruit and pastries.

First order of business, Heather decided as she poured herself a cup of tea, was to figure out the rules and traditions of Lengroth Castle. If she wanted to achieve anything here it would be a hundred times easier with Mrs Peterson on her side, and Mrs Peterson seemed to value things being done the right way.

Heather dreaded to think what Mrs Peterson would say when she discovered the real reason she'd come to Lengroth...

Secondly, she needed to remind Cal about the laptops, and money for school supplies. And clothes—much as she hated to rely on him for those. It felt too much like being paid off after sleeping with Ross.

But he was her employer; he had a responsibility towards her that had nothing to do with his brother. Maybe she could think of it as him providing her with a uniform—that might help.

Before she could get to point three on her to-do list—or to the plate of pastries—Cal looked up and caught her eye briefly before looking away.

Was he embarrassed about their middle-of-the-night conversation—argument, really?

'The laptops you asked for will be arriving this afternoon, Miss Reid. Sorry I couldn't get them here any sooner.'

So we're back to Miss Reid, then. That didn't bode well, even if the laptops did.

'That's much sooner than I expected. Thank you...' She trailed off, unsure of what to call him. Mr Bryce? Cal? My Lord—except he wasn't the Earl, was he? What was the etiquette here?

Something else to figure out, Heather supposed.

'And I've ordered a credit card for your use. In the meantime...' He reached into his pocket and pulled out his wallet. Removing a card from it, he handed it down the table to her. 'This should serve to get you started online.'

Mrs Peterson's eyebrows were so high Heather was half-afraid they might float off into the rafters of the dining hall. Apparently Cal didn't do this for all his nannies, then.

But she was different. Because he knew she had to stay. Or he was bribing her to stay, to stave off a scandal. Heather wasn't sure which one it was any more.

Confused, she took the card and tucked it securely into the pocket of her cardigan. Somehow she was going to have to figure all this out, save the children, and then sort out her own future and her baby's. But definitely not until after breakfast.

Helping herself to pastries, she turned to smile at the children, who stared sullenly back. The shadows under Daisy's eyes were grey smudges, and made her look paler and more gaunt than she already was. Ryan picked miserably at his bowl of cereal.

Start there, she decided. *Everything else can wait a few days at least. The kids need me now.*

Did they know about the sort of things their father had got up to? She hoped not. As she also hoped that Cal was right that the family were good at keeping their secrets. Daisy and Ryan didn't deserve the gossipy taunts and comments that she'd suffered as a child because of her mother's behaviour.

'So, kids… If the laptops aren't arriving until this afternoon we've got one last morning of freedom before lessons start. What would you like to spend it doing?'

Daisy and Ryan exchanged one of their secret looks, then turned to smile eerily identical smiles at Heather.

Heather swallowed. Suddenly she was regretting asking.

Cal looked up in amusement as Heather asked the fateful question. Really, as a teacher, surely she should know better than to give two devil children a *choice* in what they wanted to do next. Hell, he knew nothing about kids except how to avoid them—and even *he* knew that much.

At the far end of the table Mrs Peterson was watching, too, and Cal was sure he detected a hint of a smile around her thin lips. Old Peterson had been with the family since before Cal was born, but he could still count the number of times he'd seen her smile on both hands.

She knew all the family secrets, his mother used to say. Which was why she had a job for life. It was impossible to keep *anything* from Mrs Peterson.

Cal wondered if she'd known about Ross and the sort of man he really was. He almost hoped not. Mrs Peterson had doted on his brother, and he'd hate that to be tainted the way his own relationship with him had.

'We'd like to show you the village,' Daisy said, with total innocence in her voice. If a person didn't know her better, anyway.

But Cal knew. And he was already calculating the number of different ways the children could get into trouble.

He was up to twenty-four before Heather said, 'Lengroth village? Sure, if you like.' She sounded surprised. 'I came through it on my way here yesterday. There didn't seem to be a lot there, but maybe it'll look different with you two as my tour guides.'

She smiled warmly—a smile that only faltered slightly as Mrs Peterson said, 'I dare say it will.'

Well, whatever Daisy's cunning plan was, this would work wonderfully for Cal. With the children and Heather safely out of the castle and out of his way he could get on with the real work he still had to do. Like making another phone call to his lawyer to see what they'd made of Ross's contract with the magazine.

He was just contemplating a *pain au chocolat* to round off his breakfast before he got to work when Heather's face brightened even more, and Cal was filled with a strange sense of foreboding.

'I know! Uncle Cal can take us down to the village—it's too far to walk there *and* back, I think. Maybe we can all have some lunch together as a treat. What do you think?'

Daisy and Ryan looked as uncertain as he felt about Heather's suggestion, and Mrs Peterson was *definitely* smiling now.

But Heather ignored them all and clapped her hands together. 'Brilliant! It's a plan, then. Let's all meet at the front door in thirty minutes, ready to go.'

And with that she snatched up the last *pain au chocolat* and walked out with his breakfast, his credit card and his free morning.

Perfect.

'That's two to Miss Reid,' Mrs Peterson murmured as she cleared away his empty plate.

Cal ignored her, and went to get ready to drive down to the village.

Cal felt a strange sensation of lightening as he drove out through the front gates of Lengroth Castle, Heather in the passenger seat beside him and the children suspiciously quiet in the back seat. He was almost certain that Daisy and Ryan were plotting something, but since he had no idea what he decided to go with the flow and enjoy the day.

He was away from the castle, the sun was shining and he had a beautiful if untouchable woman at his side. Life could be much worse.

The village of Lengroth was small, mostly filled with grey stone terraced houses that echoed the castle's forbidding walls. The streets were narrow, winding up and down each side of the valley the village sat in. From every spot in the village the castle of Lengroth, up on the hill, was visible, looming over them.

Cal purposefully kept his back to it as they got out of the car.

'So, where shall we start?' Heather asked,

sounding unreasonably excited about the outing, in Cal's opinion.

'The sweet shop?' Ryan suggested hopefully.

Heather smiled. 'Maybe let's save that until after lunch. But a stroll along the high street sounds like a great idea.'

'The high street?' Cal asked, with a hint of incredulity in his voice. 'I think that title is a little grand for what Lengroth has to offer.' At most, it was a low street. It barely even qualified as a road.

Still, Heather seemed charmed as they strolled past the Mountain Ram pub and across the road by the chip shop, the corner shop—and the long-suffering Mr Reynolds' sweet shop. In fact, for just a moment Cal could almost let himself believe that they were a real family, doing real family things—not a patchwork of relatives and strangers who hardly even knew each other.

But the kids were behaving, Heather seemed relaxed and happy, and no one was demanding anything much from him, so Cal decided to relax and enjoy the rare Scottish sunshine for a change.

At least until Ryan darted across the road—narrowly missing being hit by a passing cyclist—and ran away from them down an alley.

Cal froze, just for a moment, then moved to chase him—only to find that Heather had beaten him to it. She was already across the road, disappearing through the same gap in the buildings that Ryan had, leaving him with Daisy.

He wanted to follow them, but that would mean dragging Daisy along, too—he could hardly leave her behind.

'Where would your brother be running to?' he asked, still staring after Heather.

No reply.

Annoyed, Cal turned to face Daisy—only to find her gone, too.

'Dammit.' Cal bit back a stronger curse as he spun around to check the street for his wayward niece. Nothing.

Except… A flash of movement in the distance, past the pub and behind the trees, made Cal realise he knew *exactly* where Daisy had gone.

He didn't want to go *there*. He'd been avoiding it ever since he came back to Lengroth. But apparently his niece wasn't giving him that option.

With a sigh, Cal followed her.

CHAPTER SIX

HEATHER SLIPPED DOWN the narrow alleyway, her eyes constantly moving as she searched the shadows for Ryan. What kind of nanny was she, losing one of her charges on her second day? Cal must be fuming. Or probably grilling Daisy on what Ryan thought he was playing at.

What *did* Ryan think he was playing at? It wasn't as if there were a lot of places to run away to in Lengroth, and he'd run in the opposite direction to the sweet shop so it couldn't even be that. It didn't make any sense.

Maybe he was just one of those boys who needed to run. She'd had one of those in the last school she worked at—he'd needed to escape over the fence at least once a day. The caretaker would chase him down and he'd come back, docilely enough, and go to class. But the next day it would be exactly the same.

But Ryan hadn't run yesterday. And Cal

hadn't mentioned his escaping act as one of the many problems he'd experienced with the children. Was this something new? Was he running away from *her*?

The alleyway took another turn, and Heather sighed as she rounded it—then stopped as she realised it led to a dead end.

A dead end with Ryan at the end of it, sitting calmly upon an upturned wooden crate.

He grinned impishly at her, then the smile faded. 'Where's Uncle Cal?'

'With Daisy, I hope.' Heather moved to sit on another crate opposite him, trying to make sense of exactly what was going on.

Ryan shook his head, his dark hair waving from side to side as he did so. 'No. No, no, *no*. Daisy is going to be so cross. I was supposed to lead *both* of you away. Why didn't he follow?' he asked plaintively. Then his face darkened and he answered his own question. 'It's because he can't be bothered with me and Daisy, isn't it?'

'That's not it, Ryan,' Heather said soothingly. 'One of us needed to stay with Daisy, and I was quicker than Uncle Cal, that's all.' At least she hoped that was what had happened. She hadn't dared look back to check for fear of losing Ryan's trail.

'He can't, though,' Ryan said, looking up at her with big eyes. 'He didn't want to come back to Lengroth in the first place—I heard him tell Mrs Peterson. And when you two were rowing outside our rooms last night—'

Heather winced. She'd thought he was asleep, but maybe they'd woken him up again. Sound carried surprisingly well in Lengroth Castle for a building of its size and with the thickness of its walls. 'We weren't rowing. And you weren't meant to hear that.'

'Well, I did. And I know he doesn't love us or want us. He just wants you to get us ready so he can send us away, doesn't he?'

The boy had a point, but Heather knew she couldn't concede it. 'Your uncle wants the best for your education and for your future. He's very busy with the estate right now—'

'Dad never spent so much time in his study when *he* ran the estate.'

Apparently not very well, Heather thought, but didn't say.

'Your uncle loves you,' she said firmly instead. After all, however much trouble they caused him, they were his own flesh and blood. How could he *not* love them? 'He's just not very good at showing it.' *At all. Ever.*

Ryan shook his head mulishly. 'He doesn't want us. That's okay. We don't want him, either. That's what Daisy says.'

Daisy. There was something else he'd said about Daisy, and in her relief at finding him safe she'd almost missed it. What was it...?

Heather blinked as it came to her. 'Ryan, what did you mean when you said Daisy would be cross because you were supposed to lead *both* of us away? Is this a plan you and Daisy made?'

'*Daisy's* plan,' Ryan corrected. 'They're always Daisy's plans. She just tells me what to do.'

'And today it was to run away so Cal and I would follow. But why?'

That was the part that didn't make any sense. Unless Daisy wanted to be left alone... Heather's eyes widened. Had Daisy wanted the distraction so *she* could escape, too?

'Ryan, what did Daisy need to be alone to do?'

He wouldn't meet her eyes.

Heather took several deep breaths and tried again. 'Ryan, I promise I won't be cross. And neither will Daisy.'

'Yes, she will,' he muttered, and Heather didn't try to deny it again. The boy knew his sister better than she did.

Slipping off her crate, Heather crouched in front of Ryan, her hands either side of him, looking up until he couldn't help but meet her gaze. 'Ryan, I promise you I am only here to help you. And I'm not going anywhere until you want to leave, okay? So you can trust me.'

Ryan's eyes were red around the rims, she realised. With unshed tears or lack of sleep? Or just the stress of being an eight-year-old earl whose life didn't make sense any more?

Probably all three.

'Everyone goes away—that's what Daisy says,' he whispered. 'Our parents. The nannies. And Uncle Cal will go back to America as soon as he's sent us away, too.'

The worst part was she couldn't tell him he was wrong. Shifting to perch beside him on the box, Heather put an arm around Ryan's shoulders. 'Sometimes when people go they come back again, you know.'

'Not when they're dead,' Ryan said bluntly. 'Or when you throw things at them from the nursery window.'

'Daisy threw a rubber duck at me. I stayed,' Heather pointed out. 'Even after you let me fall in the muddy riverbank.'

Ryan sneaked a quick look at her at that, a small smile on his face.

'Yeah, I guess I must have looked pretty funny,' Heather said. 'The thing is, Ryan, I can't bring your parents back—no one can. And maybe those other nannies weren't meant to stay. But I will. Until September. I promise you that. And as for Uncle Cal—'

'Don't lie to me,' Ryan said quickly. 'Don't tell me he's staying if he isn't.'

Heather sighed. 'You're right. I can't promise you anything on Uncle Cal's behalf—only he can do that. But I *can* tell you that he's doing everything he can to make sure you and Daisy have a secure future, okay? He's looking out for you, even if it doesn't feel like it.'

It wasn't enough, though, Heather knew.

These kids needed more than that. And they needed more than a detached Uncle Cal tagging along on day trips or new computers to do their schoolwork on.

Which meant she needed to have another conversation with Cal Bryce. And she was pretty sure he wasn't going to like it.

'Come on,' she said to Ryan. 'Let's go and find Daisy and Uncle Cal.'

The boy followed happily enough, apparently feeling a little better for getting some things off his chest.

It was only as they reached the high street again that Heather realised he'd never answered her question about what Daisy had wanted to be alone to do.

Cal approached the spot behind the trees slowly, quietly, not wanting to disturb Daisy as she knelt at the base of the tree stump.

Who had told her that this was where her parents had died? Had it been gossip in the town, or one of the local nannies?

Either way, she knew. And she'd wanted to come here so badly she'd sent her brother running off to cause a distraction—he was sure of it. Ryan always did do everything his big sister suggested.

Swallowing, Cal took another step forward, hating it that he was there—hating it even more that Daisy was.

The pub had fixed up the mess that had been made of their front wall, and Stan the landlord had planted some bedding plants along the new wall—green and purple, the Lengroth colours, in memory of Ross and Janey. Ross had been Stan's best customer, by all accounts.

The tree the car had hit, after it had come through the wall, had been too damaged to be saved. That had been sawn off, a foot or so from the grass, and sanded smooth. Daisy had placed something on top of the stump, Cal realised as he got closer.

He stepped on a fallen twig, snapping it loudly underfoot, and Daisy spun around, jumping to her feet.

'You followed me,' she said, as if he were in the wrong. 'You were supposed to follow Ryan.'

He'd known it had to be a plan. 'Heather followed Ryan. He'll be fine.'

'He probably hasn't gone very far anyway.' Daisy turned back to face the tree stump again. 'He's always too much of a scaredy-cat to run far.'

'You've done this before, then?' Cal moved around to the other side of the stump so he could see her face.

'All the time,' she replied nonchalantly. 'The other nannies never told you because they didn't want to get into trouble for losing Ryan. And I was always back where they'd left me before they returned with him.'

It was just as well all those other nannies had quit. He'd have fired them anyway.

'I think Heather would have told me if I hadn't been here today.'

Daisy gave him a sceptical look. So young... so cynical.

'Yeah, I'm surprised, too,' he admitted, taking a seat on the bench next to the pub wall. He patted the wood beside him, motioning for Daisy to join him. She didn't. 'So why do you keep coming back here?' he asked.

'To talk to them.'

Right. 'But why here? Most people would go to the churchyard, you know. If you want to visit their graves Heather will take you.'

Not him. The last place he wanted to be was in that churchyard, with generation after generation of Bryces and their scandals haunting him, more real than the Lengroth ghost. No, scratch that. The churchyard was the second to last place he wanted to be.

Here was the absolute last. Looking at the spot where his brother had died.

'Because this is the last place that they were alive,' Daisy said, with the simplicity and bluntness of a child. 'It's just their bodies in the ground by the church. Here is where they were last really *them.*'

'That makes sense.' Or at least, he supposed it did if you were ten. 'What is it you want to say to them?'

Daisy's face closed up. 'That's private.'

'Right.' Cal looked over at the tree stump. Sitting on top of it was Ross's old teddy bear—the one he'd kept on the top shelf in the nursery. 'I'll tell you what, then. You have your conversation and I'll go and wait by the road for your brother and Heather. Okay?'

He'd still be able to see her from the road, but not to hear her words. It was about as much privacy as he was willing to give her, under the circumstances.

Daisy weighed the idea up, glancing between him and the road, then back to the tree stump. Finally she nodded. 'Okay.'

True to his word, Cal walked out of earshot and waited by the wall, scanning the streets for Heather and Ryan. No sign yet, but if Daisy wasn't worried neither was he. High above the village loomed Lengroth Castle, with all the worries he still had to deal with inside it. That was enough worrying to be going on with, anyway.

Then he frowned as his gaze followed the road down the hill from the castle to the wall he leaned against, moved past the memorial flowers and to Daisy, by the tree stump.

It's the wrong way round, he realised suddenly.

Mrs Peterson had told him that Ross and Janey had been returning to the castle in the early hours of the morning, after some party or another, when they'd crashed. Ross had been over the limit, so Janey had been driving—and she had never liked to drive at night.

It had sounded plausible, so he'd never questioned it. And he'd never felt the need to return to the scene of the accident, as Daisy obviously did. But now he was here he saw what was wrong with the story.

For the car to have hit the wall, and then the tree, it must have been driving *away* from the castle—not towards it.

Where were you going, Ross? And why?

Cal shook his head. Another puzzle for him to try and make sense of.

A flash of movement across the road caught his eye and he saw Heather waving at him as she and Ryan walked towards him. He waved back, tucking away his questions about his brother to think about later, when he was alone.

First he needed to deal with his niece and nephew. Not to mention their nanny.

'You run to Daisy,' Heather whispered to Ryan as they got closer. 'Leave Uncle Cal to me.'

She'd been terrified for a moment when she'd seen Cal standing alone by the pub wall, but then Ryan had gasped and she'd seen Daisy, just beyond him, talking to a tree stump.

Why she'd needed to send her brother running off so she could do that, Heather had no idea. But she was sure she would find out soon enough.

Once they were safely across the road, Ryan dashed over to his sister and Heather moved more slowly to stand beside Cal.

'Don't shout at him for running off,' she said before he could speak. 'He already thinks you can't wait to get rid of him, so don't make things worse. I've already spoken to him on the walk back about not running away any more.'

Cal didn't even flinch at her words, which made it worse somehow. Ryan was right; he *didn't* want the responsibility of the children. But now he had it she was going to make damn sure he realised how lucky he was to have them—and how his responsibility stretched far beyond their financial futures.

She had no patience for people who walked out on their obligations to their children.

'He did it for Daisy,' he said, surprising her. She hadn't expected him to realise that.

'It was a plan. She wanted to visit the place where their parents died, and Ryan distracted you so she could slip away here. Apparently they've done it to all the other nannies.'

Heather winced, looking over at the two children together by the tree stump. 'Those poor kids.'

'Yeah. Apparently none of the other nannies told me about Ryan's running away because they thought they'd get into trouble.'

He gave her a look she couldn't quite read.

'You'd have told me, right? If I hadn't been here?'

'Yes.' Because it would have been the right thing to do. He was their guardian, and he deserved to know what was happening in their lives. And because it might have prompted him to take slightly more interest in their emotional well-being.

'Good.' Cal glanced up towards the castle, frowning. Obviously he was still thinking about whatever paperwork or accounts he'd left undone that morning, rather than about the children in his care.

Heather opened her mouth to tell him what she thought of that, but then Daisy and Ryan appeared. Daisy was holding a teddy bear Heather hadn't noticed on their way into town. She must have been hiding it under her summer jacket.

'Can we go to the bakery and get sausage rolls for lunch?' Ryan asked, seemingly unaffected by their visit to the spot where his parents died.

Heather supposed that in the end it was just another place. Although it seemed that it meant more than that to Daisy.

She really needed to talk to Daisy.

After she'd straightened Cal's priorities out, anyway.

'Yes, we can get sausage rolls,' Heather agreed. 'And then go back to the castle. We've got work to be getting on with.'

Daisy was silent all through the sausage roll eating and the drive back to the castle. She was even silent through the discovery of the three laptops that had arrived for them while they were out.

Ryan, apparently more comfortable around Heather since their talk that morning, happily chatted and asked questions as she set the laptops up, plugging two of them in to charge at the desks in the playroom next to the kids' bedrooms. For now, it would have to double as a classroom, too.

Daisy, meanwhile, sat on the window seat pretending to read. Heather knew she was only pretending, because she'd forgotten to turn any pages for the last twenty minutes. Plus, she was staring at her and Ryan.

'Right—here we go,' Heather said eventually, as she got the evaluation website she'd chosen up and running on both the kids' laptops.

Ryan leaned in closer, manoeuvring himself onto the seat at his desk without ever taking his eyes off the screen. Daisy ignored her.

Heather held in a sigh. 'Daisy? Would you come over here, please?'

With a considerable amount of eye-rolling, and slamming the book closed, Daisy crossed the room to join them at the two desks.

'Before I can start teaching you I need to know how much you've already learned,' Heather explained as Daisy took her seat. 'So, what I would like you to do this afternoon is work your way through the questions on the screens—I've started you off on the ones that are appropriate for your ages.'

A tiny fib; she'd actually started them both one stage lower. That way they wouldn't be intimidated if they found it a little tricky, and if they flew through them they'd feel better about themselves—and hopefully the idea of education in general.

'The questions will keep coming until you reach a point where the programme thinks it has fully assessed your levels, and then it will tell you you're done. And when it's finished we're done for the day, too. I figured we could play a game afterwards, or go for an early-evening walk before dinner. Just not by the river,' she added, and Ryan flashed her a grin.

She was definitely making progress with Ryan.

'So, basically, this is your way of teaching us without you having to do any work,' Daisy said. 'What are *you* going to be doing while we sit here doing tests?'

Daisy not so much.

'I am going to go and have a conversation with your uncle about your programme of study.' Which sounded a lot better than *I'm going to yell at Cal until he at least tries to connect with you both, so you don't have to go visiting your dead parents for love and affection.*

'So you won't even be in the *room* while we're doing this!'

Daisy sounded incredulous at the unfairness of life. Heather would have thought she'd have been used to it by now.

'Aren't you afraid we're going to cheat?' Ryan asked curiously.

Heather got the impression that trust hadn't been a big factor in their education before now.

'I trust you both to take this seriously,' she said, and watched as Ryan's shoulders straightened with pride. Daisy, however, had a scheming gleam in her eye.

'Besides,' Heather went on with a shrug, 'these tests are to judge the level of work I'm going to set you from here on. If you cheat to do better then you'll get work that's too hard. If you pretend you're stupid to get easier work I guarantee you'll be bored stiff by the end of the week. So really it's up to you.'

Daisy's gleam faded.

'I'll wait until I'm certain you're both happy with the software. So, if you're both ready?' Heather asked. 'You can begin.'

And she could get to work on her real challenge—Cal Bryce.

CHAPTER SEVEN

CAL DIDN'T REALISE he'd been waiting for the knock on his study door until he heard it. His shoulders tensed as he called, 'Come in.'

Heather's copper curls appeared around the door first, followed by the rest of her.

'Miss Reid,' he said, and she scowled. 'Sorry—Heather.'

'I need to talk to you about the children.'

'I need to talk to you about them, too,' he countered, motioning to the seat on the other side of his desk.

There was no rubber duck on the desk between them this time. Cal had a strange feeling that it might have made things easier if there was.

'Where are they, for a start?' he asked as she sat.

'Taking some online quizzes to help me assess their level of learning,' Heather replied.

'And, no, that isn't just so I don't have to teach them anything this afternoon.'

That sounded like a Daisy accusation if ever he'd heard one. 'Aren't you afraid that they'll cheat with you out of the room?'

Heather gave him a curious look—one that didn't quite make sense in the context of his question. A look that made Cal feel decidedly uncomfortable.

'No, I'm not afraid they'll cheat,' she said.

Cal tore his gaze away from her inquisitive one and shuffled the papers in front of him back into their folder. He didn't want Heather to see the annotated copy of Ross's contract with the magazine his lawyer, Graham, had sent over. In fact, he wasn't even sure *he* wanted to see it. Graham hadn't sounded particularly happy about it when he'd called.

'So, what do you want to talk about?' he asked, pushing the whole magazine thing to the back of his mind. He had more important things to worry about right now, anyway. Like Heather and the children.

He frowned suddenly. When had *they* become more important than the business of Lengroth Castle? Because that definitely wasn't the natural order of things in the Bryce family.

The words burst out from Heather in a tirade, and he realised quickly how much she'd been holding back all morning.

'Here's the thing. I know you think you're looking after Ross's children by taking care of their financial futures and stability, and by making sure they get a good education. But that's not enough. And it's not what they need right now. They're grieving, they're struggling, and they need a hell of a lot more from you than a good investment portfolio.'

Since Cal was mostly aiming for not bankrupting the estate in paying off Ross's debts, Heather's assessment seemed a little optimistic, but he took the point. Well, mostly…

'This is what I can do for them,' he said. 'And this *does* matter.'

Heather rolled her eyes. 'Yes, fine—it matters. But what good is it going to do them if they're so screwed up by their childhood that they go off the rails before they're eighteen and blow through their inheritance in a fortnight the moment they get it?'

Cal froze at her words. Heather couldn't know it, but she was describing the life cycle of the average Bryce male right there. How had he never seen that before? Yes, their tendency towards scandal and self-destruction might be bred into the genes, but it wasn't *only* there. It was learned, too.

It was too late for Ross, and probably too late for Cal, too. But maybe it wasn't too late for Ryan and Daisy.

Obviously encouraged by his stunned silence, Heather went on. 'They need more than a nanny and a good boarding school, Cal. They've lost their parents—you saw what lengths they went to today just to feel close to them again. They've closed off until they only have each other. They don't believe anyone will stay—that's why they've been driving the nannies away. Well, them and the ghost, I suppose...'

'But *you'll* stay,' Cal said. 'Won't you?'

She met his gaze, her eyes a wonderful bright green against her pale skin. Like summer leaves, full of life and vibrancy.

'Yes. I'll stay.'

There was a promise in her words, a truth he could rely on, and Cal realised that he trusted her in a way he hadn't trusted anyone since Ross. Since he was a child who hadn't known any better.

Heather would stay.

If there were no other truths and hard facts in the world *that* at least he was sure of. Whatever happened to Lengroth and the estate finances, and the children and boarding school, and even that damn ghost, Heather was one of them now. Tied in through a baby no one had expected or wanted until it was growing inside her and Heather had decided to love it anyway.

Because that was the sort of person she was. He'd only known her two days but Cal knew that already. Heather was good and honest and true and faithful. She'd said she would stay, so she would.

And even if a large part of his brain was telling Cal that he should send her away…set her free from Lengroth before the Bryce family ruined her the way they ruined everything else… Cal knew he wouldn't do it.

Not because she looked beautiful when she was feeling righteous about something, or because she'd shown up with a rubber duck under her arm to tell him about her night with Ross because it was 'the right thing'. Not even because she was pregnant with Ross's child, and the only nanny who stood a chance of sticking it out with Daisy and Ryan.

But because Lengroth Castle—and more specifically his niece and nephew—needed an infusion of that goodness if they ever wanted to stand a chance of breaking the cycle of destruction and pain in the future.

'But if I'm staying, Cal—'

'Which you are,' he interrupted quickly, in case she'd changed her mind while he was ruminating.

'Then I need you to support me with the children.'

'I told you—laptops, books, whatever you need,' he said quickly. 'Money is no object.' He might have depleted his own personal funds significantly to pay off Ross's debts, but that didn't mean he was exactly hard up compared to the rest of the population. He could afford whatever it took to help Heather fix his niece and nephew. And there were always investments he could cash in if it proved necessary.

Soon Lengroth would be back on its feet and the estate would repay everything he'd invested. At least that was the plan.

But Heather shook her head. 'This isn't about money, Cal. It's about *you*.'

He stared blankly at her and she sighed.

'They need more than *things*,' she explained. 'They've lost their parents—they've lost love and faith and their trust in the world. They need their new guardian to step up and fill that gap. They need you to love them and show them that. Every single day.'

'Love?'

Money, he could do. Love... He had no idea how *that* would work.

'Love,' Heather said again, more firmly. 'You're their only parent now, Cal, like it or not. Which means you need to be mother and father to them. You need to show them that they're safe and loved and that they can come to you when they need help, or when they're scared or lonely, or just because they need a hug.'

Cal shook his head. Love was too abstract—too far removed from his experiences in this castle. But Heather was right—Daisy and Ryan were his responsibility now, and if this was what they needed he had to find a way to give that to them. As much as he'd like to hand the whole thing over to Heather to fix, that wouldn't work long-term. Yes, she was staying—but only until September. After that it would be boarding school and Lengroth Castle in the holidays for years to come.

He needed to find a way to make that work. And if he didn't want Daisy and Ryan to end up like the rest of them he had to do it fast.

Cal ran Heather's words back in his head. *'Show them that they're safe and loved.'* But how? How was he supposed to do that?

He caught Heather's steady green gaze across the desk and realised the answer was right in front of him.

He smiled. 'Fine. But if you want me to do those things the kids aren't the only ones you're going to have to teach.'

* * *

Heather blinked. When her eyes opened again Cal was still looking at her, a faint smirk on his lips.

'Teach?' Was this some sort of bizarre come-on? What was she missing here?

'I need kid lessons,' Cal clarified with a shrug. 'I've never had children—never spent much time with them before. I have literally no idea how to do what you're asking. So if you want me to do it you'll have to teach me how.'

'Teach you how to...*love*?' Who didn't know how to love another person? Especially a child?

Apart from my mother.

Except even that wasn't fair, or true, and Heather told herself off in her head for even thinking it. Her mother not being able to love hadn't been the problem. Quite the reverse, really. Even if she *had* left her husband and only child behind because of it, to live with the consequences for ever.

'Exactly,' Cal replied, as if it was the most obvious thing in the world.

Heather chewed her bottom lip as she thought

about it. Love wasn't something that could be taught, was it? It was just…natural.

But children—their needs and the way they understood the world—parenting skills and techniques…they were all things a person could take courses in or read books on. *They* could be taught, in a way. She'd studied class-room discipline and how to relate to students, to help and support them, before she'd quali-fied as a teacher. Although the best lesson was always just standing up in front of a class and having to *do* it…

She smiled. Yes, she could teach Cal from books and studies. But the biggest part of his education would come from spending time with Daisy and Ryan. And *that* was what would help him learn to fall in love with them. She was certain of it.

They might be prickly and difficult, but un-derneath that spiky outer shell Heather was sure that they were good kids. Ryan was al-ready starting to come out of his shell, and Heather had hopes that Daisy wouldn't be too far behind. Having their uncle spending more time with them could only help with that.

'Okay,' she said, and watched as Cal visibly relaxed. 'We'll start tonight.'

By the time she made it back to the nursery both children had completed the tests she'd set them and were investigating their new computers—and presumably the comprehensive child security software she'd put in place.

'How did you find the tests?' she asked, settling into the window seat as they reluctantly closed their laptops. At least Uncle Cal had already done one thing to win their favour, even if they mostly had to use them for schoolwork.

Daisy shrugged. 'They were boring. But fine.'

'Yeah, easy,' Ryan agreed, shooting his sister a look. But his words didn't sound as sure as Daisy's.

Heather made a mental note to review their scores with them individually. Ryan seemed far more likely to open up to her and speak the truth if his big sister wasn't there.

Summer rain had started to fall outside while they were working, and after their outing that morning Heather was suddenly reluctant to let them outside the grounds again that day anyway. So instead she pulled a board game down from the shelf, ignoring Daisy's groan of complaint, and they settled down to play it together.

As they played Heather found herself watching them and looking for signs of their father and uncle in them. Hearing Cal echoing Ryan's words about her worrying about them cheating had started her thinking about Cal's own childhood. Hearing him state so baldly that he'd have to be taught how to love the children… well, that only confirmed her suspicions that growing up in Lengroth Castle couldn't have been the warmest of experiences.

But maybe she could help change that for Ryan and Daisy. They'd be half-siblings to her own baby, after all. Which made them family. And Heather believed in family almost more than anything else in this world.

Which was why she had to help Cal see that, too.

After a gloating Daisy won the game, then retreated to her own bedroom with a book, Heather set Ryan up with some vaguely educational games on the laptop, then pulled out her own computer to do some work.

After heading a new document *Lessons in Childcare and Love*, she started to type.

Cal wanted to learn? Then she was more than ready to teach.

Cal was already regretting his request for kid lessons even *before* Heather showed up with a neatly typed syllabus, a reading list and a print-out of study findings from the last five years.

'You expect me to do assigned reading?' he asked, incredulous, as he scanned the papers.

'You wanted to learn,' she replied with a shrug.

Rubbing a hand across his aching forehead, Cal flipped through the syllabus instead. 'What are these?' he asked, pointing to the sections that were colour-coded in green. Of *course* it was colour-coded. He didn't know why he'd expected differently. 'Practical modules?'

'Those are the times you take the kids out and spend time with them.'

'On my *own*?' Cal winced as he heard how high and squeaky his voice had grown on the last word.

Heather shrugged. 'Maybe not to start with.

But eventually, yes. You're their *parent* now, remember? The only person they have.'

As if he could forget.

Sighing, he sank down into the same armchair he'd sat in every night since he'd arrived at Lengroth, trying to figure out how to save the place and get it back on its feet before Ryan turned eighteen and took it over. This little sitting room, just off the kitchen, was the warmest room in the house in the winter, but cool and shady in the summer. It had a well-stocked drinks cabinet, a speaker system Ross had installed a couple of years before, and some of his favourite books in the whole castle on its shelves.

If Cal had to stay in Lengroth Castle at least he could use some of the comforts of the place to make it a little more bearable. And since it looked from Heather's syllabus as if he'd be there a long time…

'Maybe we should get a castle dog…' he mused as Heather sat down across from him, in the same chair she'd chosen the night before.

That was nice. They were finding little routines and habits already. Things that might make the summer stretch less dauntingly ahead of him.

Heather rolled her eyes. 'A dog—faithful companion and lovely pet that it is—can't be a replacement for a parent's time and affection, Cal.'

'I wasn't actually thinking of the children,' Cal admitted with an embarrassed smile. 'Although it might not be a bad idea. We always had dogs here when we were kids, Ross and I.'

They'd been the perfect companions. Friendly, affectionate—and they'd never shared any of the secrets he'd sobbed out to them in the dark of the night, alone in his room.

Heather was studying him again, he realised. 'What?'

'I was just wondering...what was it like, growing up here? With Ross?'

Was she asking because she wanted to know more about his brother? Or because she was trying to figure out what it must be like for Daisy and Ryan? Or maybe...just because she cared?

Cal looked away from those bright green eyes that always seemed to see just a little too much.

'It was…difficult. Our parents had firm ideas about the aristocracy and our place in it, and the obligations that brought with it.'

Heather nodded seriously as she said, 'I imagine they expected a certain standard of behaviour from you both, knowing that the world would be paying more attention to the sons of an earl than to just us normal folk.'

Cal barked out a harsh laugh, one that hurt even his own ears and made Heather wince. 'Sorry. I just… Yes, you're right. To a point.'

'To a point?'

Her head tilted to the left again and he wondered suddenly if she'd purposefully led him down this path to revelations. However they'd got there, he wanted to backtrack.

'We're not here to talk about my childhood. We're here to talk about Daisy and Ryan's.'

'True.' Heather shuffled the stack of paper in her hands—even larger than the binder of clipped pages she'd given him. 'Let's get started, then.'

Cal tried to listen as she talked about recent studies and best practice and a child's need for attention. But his mind wouldn't focus. He felt as if he was drifting back twenty years and her words faded away to a hum at the back of his mind.

Because the rest of him was a child again, trying to survive within the cold and loveless walls of Lengroth Castle.

'The strange thing is, our impulse is to believe that shouting at children, punishing them—giving them negative attention, basically—will drive them away from the behaviour that caused it,' Heather said. 'But actually the opposite is often true. If a child isn't getting high-quality, regular and predictable time and attention from a parent or guardian or whoever, then they'll take whatever attention they can get—however negative. So rewarding bad behaviour with attention of any sort can actually just make the child do it more.'

Rewarding bad behaviour. Was that the problem the Bryce family had? No matter how badly they behaved they only seemed to be rewarded for it—with lands and estates and money and attention in glossy magazines like the one Ross had that bloody contract with.

Except, no. Because those rewards relied on

nobody ever finding out about all the scandals and cruelty. Their high station had just made it easier for them to get away with things.

Like Ross had done for so long.

But Ross had to have been a better father than their own had been, right? Cal felt sure about that much, at least. Ross would never have beaten a child. Would never have threatened to slit his dog's throat in front of him at the dinner table for some imagined or perceived slight against him.

Would he?

Cal swallowed as he remembered the reason he'd never had a pet dog as an adult. Not after what had happened to Cavall, the night of the worst of his father's rages...

'Cal?'

Heather had put her papers down on the table beside her chair. When had she done that? When had she stopped talking? He wasn't sure.

He shook his head. 'Sorry. I was just... remembering.'

'Growing up here?' she asked softly, and he nodded.

She bit her lower lip, a habit he'd noticed last

night in the hallway and something that had previously made his pulse kick up a gear just at the sight of it. But tonight his heart was already racing from memories, and Heather's lips couldn't compete with them. *Quite.*

'I think… Cal, I think that if you want to learn how to take care of Daisy and Ryan we need to talk about some other stuff first. Okay?'

Cal reached for the bottle of brandy beside his table. 'There's nothing to talk about.'

'Right. Except…you know…*everything.*' She gave him an apologetic smile. 'Look, if it makes you feel better I'll go first.'

'Go first?'

She shrugged. 'You know… I'll show you my childhood trauma if you show me yours.'

Cal paused halfway through taking the lid off the brandy bottle to pour himself a glass. 'Your childhood trauma?' He couldn't imagine Heather having anything except the kind of perfect, idyllic childhood he'd read about in storybooks before he was old enough to accept the world as it really was.

'We all have one, right? So… Pour me a drink—non-alcoholic, please—and I'll begin.'

Slowly he leaned across to select a second glass, then found the bottle of elderflower cordial. There was no way he intended to share his childhood at Lengroth with anyone. But he wanted to know what kind of childhood had made Heather the way she was. Especially since it couldn't be anything like his own and Ross's.

Maybe then he could learn how to make Daisy and Ryan's better, too.

'Tell me.'

CHAPTER EIGHT

HEATHER'S HANDS SHOOK at the very idea of sharing her past with this man. But if it was the only way to get Cal to open up about his own childhood then it was the right thing to do. For Daisy and for Ryan—and maybe even for Cal himself.

Taking the glass of elderflower cordial from him, Heather allowed herself a small sip before she started talking.

'I grew up in a little Hertfordshire village,' she started. 'You know the sort—where everyone knows everyone else and all their business.'

'Sounds like Lengroth. Well, mostly,' Cal amended.

She wondered what that amendment was for. She could well imagine how difficult it must have been for Cal and Ross, growing up in a small community where everyone would have been watching them even more closely than most young boys, waiting for them to screw up or do something worth reporting back to the Earl—or the newspapers.

'Anyway, my father was leader of the village council, and he ran the post office and corner shop on the high street, and my mother was a teacher at the nearest secondary school.'

They might not have had aristocratic status, but her parents' jobs and roles in the community had made them more than high-profile enough for Heather's liking.

'So far so idyllic,' Cal commented. 'Go on.'

What came next? The fall from grace, of course. The point where everything had gone wrong. But the words stuck in Heather's throat even as she pushed herself to say them. She'd never needed to tell anyone this story before. Either they already knew it or they had no need ever to hear it.

Until now.

'My mother…she taught the sixth form, mostly. Seventeen- and eighteen-year-olds.' Heather swallowed. 'She fell in love with one of her students—a seventeen-year-old boy. Only seven years older than I was. They started an affair.'

With a wince, Cal topped up her elderflower cordial.

She took another gulp. 'They got caught, of course. In the classroom, in fact, by the head teacher. The news was around the village before she'd even made it home to tell Dad.'

'What happened next?' Cal asked.

She could hear the tension in his words. He obviously knew it wouldn't be good. 'Mum was suspended from her job immediately, of course. His parents talked about pressing charges. But the boy—John, he was called...'

Oh, hell, her eyes were burning now. Could she blame the pregnancy hormones for the tears on her cheeks? Probably not.

'He told everyone who would listen that they were in love. That Mum loved him far more than her husband or me. Mum...she said it wasn't true. That John had made it all up— that it was all a misunderstanding and there was nothing between them.'

'And was it untrue?'

'No. But even after everyone knew she kept on lying. Until…'

Cal's eyes fluttered closed, as if he were feeling her pain. Heather was just glad he wasn't looking at her as she told him the rest of the sordid tale.

'Two nights later they ran away together. Just disappeared in the middle of the night. I… We never heard from Mum again. Not in the last eighteen years.'

Cal's eyes flew open. 'Never? She didn't leave a note or anything?'

Heather shrugged. 'She did. Just a short letter, saying she was sorry, but she loved John and that was more important than anything.'

'How did your dad take it?'

'Badly.' Which might be the biggest understatement of the year. 'He was destroyed. He loved her so much, and it broke him when he realised she loved someone else.'

Broke *her*, too—not that she intended to mention that. Cal already had the pitying look in his eyes that she'd grown so used to seeing from the villagers. Well, the ones who weren't giving her knowing looks and talking behind her back, anyway.

'He started drinking,' she went on. 'Lost his place on the council, his reputation... Almost lost the shop, too. People felt sorry for him, of course, but the scandal was too juicy for them to resist gossiping about it. He grew paranoid, started thinking everyone was talking about him all the time. He'd be walking down the street and he'd hear someone say something, and then he'd be yelling at them, threatening them—all sorts. It was...horrible.'

Another understatement.

'And now?' Cal asked. 'How is he now?'

'Better.' Heather attempted a smile. 'Much better. Eventually he landed himself in enough trouble that his doctor insisted on counselling, and that helped, I think. But he still can't bear to talk about her, or hear her name. He took down all her photos, but... I look just like her, you see.'

Cal's expression turned stony. 'He took it out on you?'

'No!' Heather's eyes widened. 'No, my dad loves me. It was never... No. Not that. But I don't think it made it any easier for him, having me there as a daily reminder.'

He'd tried so hard never to let on, bless him. But Heather had always known when he got that faraway look in his eye, watching her, that he was thinking of her mother.

'So. Not quite so idyllic, then,' Cal said.

He was watching her carefully, Heather noted as she wiped a stray tear from her cheek. Watching her responses, her reactions. His, however, seemed strangely absent. As if the story that had defined her whole life was more of an amusing anecdote than a tragedy. Apart from when he'd thought her father had hurt her, he'd been emotionless throughout the whole thing.

Heather was almost afraid of what that said about his own story.

She shrugged. 'Not perfect, no. But it could have been worse. My father loves me, and that counts for a lot. He did his best by me once the worst of it was over.' And she did her best by him in return. They were family, after all. They had to stick together. 'Growing up without Mum…that was awful. But it was her choice.'

'But not one you would ever have made?' Cal said quietly.

'No.' Heather's hands went protectively to her stomach. Her baby was barely more than a cluster of cells, and already she couldn't imagine ever leaving it. 'The worst part—well, no, not the worst part, but the part that lingered the longest—was the gossip. The scandal. I'll for ever be the girl whose mother ran off with a student and left her behind. People can't look at me and see past that once they know.'

'I can,' Cal said, and she knew he believed it.

She gave him a small smile. 'Wait and see.'

He looked away. 'I'm sorry that happened to you.'

'People grow up with worse,' Heather replied. She bit her lip and took a chance. 'In fact, I'm almost certain that *you* did.'

He met her gaze with a crooked smile. 'Is that a subtle hint that it's my turn to share my pain?'

'If you want to tell me,' Heather replied, settling back in her chair.

The only problem was, as much as she knew she needed to hear it—for Daisy and Ryan's sake—she wasn't at all sure she wanted to. She already felt too close to this man. Had shared more than she'd meant to. It was as if she could feel the room—hell, the *world*—growing smaller around them, until they were all that mattered.

When she knew his truths, his secrets, how much harder would it be to pull back again? But all the same... She needed to know.

'Tell me,' she repeated.

And Cal began to talk.

'Tell me.'

She'd said it as if it were nothing at all—a story round a campfire. As if there should be marshmallows. As if it wasn't generations of secrets he was letting out.

Why should he tell her? Why not just lie? Make up a slightly awkward childhood filled with minor issues and small hurts? Pretend, the way every member of his family had for hundreds of years, that they were upstanding, respectable people?

But then he met her steady green gaze and knew that he would tell her everything.

What *was* this hold she had over him? It was

as if her goodness, her determination to do the right thing, was lashing him to her morals.

Because he wanted so badly to be more like her. To have less of the Bryce blood and darkness in him.

Because he wanted to believe that he could give that to Daisy and Ryan. Make their future brighter than their family's past.

But only if he told the truth now.

'My family...the Bryce family...they've held land and power and influence here for hundreds and hundreds of years. And their reputation has always been...impeccable. No scandal, no mistresses, no illegitimate children.'

Heather winced at that one—understandably.

'No financial difficulties, not even a servant dismissed under suspicious circumstances. Even more recently there's never been a photo of any Bryce falling out of a taxi, drunk at a nightclub, and no Bryce woman has ever worn the wrong thing to a royal wedding. Bryce men fought in all the wars like they were supposed to. Bryce women dutifully gave an heir and a spare to every generation. The family here at Lengroth Castle are purer than pure, whiter than white—the pinnacle of what the aristocracy should be. Looked up to throughout the land.'

'And we need to keep it that way, son,' his father had always told him.

Even now Cal knew he was living the Bryce legacy—keeping Heather here, where she couldn't let on about what his brother had done. Keeping the scandal close so it couldn't get out.

Although, now he knew about her mother, he knew for certain that she'd never tell. She'd never want to bring another scandal down on herself—or her father. And the illegitimate child of an earl who had died under what even Cal now had to admit were suspicious circumstances…that would definitely count as a scandal.

He looked over at her, another wave of guilt crashing over him as he thought about what Ross had done to her. If nothing else, he'd upended her life. And Cal hadn't exactly helped with that, either, forcing her to stay here at Lengroth for the summer.

Heather, meanwhile, looked sympathetic but

confused. 'I can see how that level of perfection would be—'

'No,' he interrupted, anger flaring that she should believe it even for a moment. She'd met Ross, after all. She knew more of the truth than most. 'The problem is that it's all a pack of lies.'

'Oh.' Heather gave him a small smile. 'I'll admit I was wondering where Ross fitted into that picture.'

Cal ran his hands through his hair with a chuckle. 'Ironically, Ross was the one I thought was different. I thought he'd broken the Bryce curse. That he had the perfect happy marriage and the perfect happy children. Then I came home after his death and found all of this.'

He cast his hands around him, hoping the movement would encompass both the castle, the kids, the debts, Heather's baby—and that damn contract upstairs in his study.

'How bad is it here?' Heather asked. 'Really? You mentioned that the finances aren't as healthy as you'd like...'

Cal sighed. 'That's just part of it. The next logical step for the whole Bryce legacy, I suppose. Ross has run this place almost into the ground—huge gambling debts, obligations to people and companies he'd obviously made to try and buy himself some more time to get the money together. I can cover the financial stuff myself—one of the benefits of being the younger son has been spending the last decade getting out of the shadow of Lengroth and making my own way in the world. I've had enough success that the money isn't too much of a problem.'

'But you didn't count on the scandal of an extra illegitimate child to throw into the mix,' Heather murmured. 'And we haven't even talked about how we're going to tell Daisy and Ryan the truth about that, when it's time.'

'Or *if* we are.'

That was his Bryce blood rising up again. The instinct to hide from scandal, to pretend none of it had ever happened, wish it away. But he couldn't pretend Heather didn't exist. And, heaven help him, he didn't want to wish her away.

He shoved that thought down. As if the situation wasn't bad enough as it was. The last thing he needed to do was develop *feelings* of any kind for the woman carrying his brother's illegitimate child.

'The thing I learned about scandal from my mother,' Heather said softly, 'is that it always comes out in the end. If she'd told my father the truth up front…managed the situation properly…maybe everything wouldn't have been as awful as it was. But because she lied everything was a hundred times worse.'

It was hard to imagine a teacher and student relationship like that *ever* ending particularly well, but Cal didn't mention it. He knew what she was really saying.

'We'll talk about it,' he promised. 'Add it to the list.'

'Speaking of which… You've told me about Ross as an adult. But what about when you were children? And when you say your family's reputation was all a pack of lies, that's not just Ross, is it? So…what's the truth?'

He looked away before he answered, as if he couldn't meet her eyes while admitting to it. God, how bad was it? She'd known Ross was no saint, but Cal seemed upstanding and re-

spectable—apart from his lack of understanding about love. How bad could the rest of his
family have been?

'In every generation Bryce men have cheated,
gambled, drunk, caused pain and suffering and
humiliation. They're just better at covering it
up than most people.'

'Okay…' That sounded bad, obviously. But a
lot of people drank too much or spent too much
on the horses. Her own father had succumbed
for a time. She leaned forward, towards Cal.
'When you say pain and suffering…?'

'I mean it,' Cal said openly. 'My father…
Ross used to stand in front of me to protect me
from his fists, his belt or just his knife-edged
tongue. But he always found a way around
eventually—unless he was too drunk to stand
up. You know why I can find the kids when
none of the nannies can? Because I know every
damn hiding place in this castle. I remember
cowering in the nook behind that hanging by
the main staircase while my father bellowed
for me—until he got so mad at my hiding he
threw my dog down the stairs in front of me
and broke his neck.'

Heather shuddered and reached out towards him, desperate to offer some comfort if she could. But Cal pulled back before she could touch him.

'I still didn't come out from behind that hanging. I slept there until Ross found me—after midnight.'

'Cal, I'm so sorry.'

No wonder he thought he couldn't love the children like a father. He'd had no example of it, no way to learn—except from the older brother he'd clearly idolised, but who had turned out to be flawed, too.

'Your father sounds…terrible. But that doesn't mean that every man in your family is like that. Ross wasn't—was he? I know he wasn't exactly faithful…'

'He never hit the kids, as far as I know, if that's what you're asking.'

Heather let out a breath of relief. She'd dealt with abused kids before, and hadn't thought that Daisy and Ryan showed any signs of that at least, but as a teacher she knew a person could never be totally sure.

'I only knew Ross for one night, and heaven

knows I realise he had failings. But he didn't seem like a cruel or unloving man.'

'He was cheating on his wife and lying to you *and* her about it,' Cal pointed out.

'You have a point,' Heather admitted grimly. 'But his bad behaviour—or your father's—doesn't mean that your whole family is bad.'

Or that Cal was incapable of giving Daisy and Ryan the family they needed—because she was almost certain that was what *Cal* thought.

'You're not listening. It wasn't just Ross, or our father. It's every Bryce man *ever.*' Cal looked up suddenly, his eyes wide and feverish. 'You know that damn ghost that all the nannies claimed to be running from? She was a servant here, a hundred years ago or so. Story is she got into trouble with a stable hand and lost her footing on the stairs trying to run away and elope with him. Crashed her head open on the stone steps.'

Heather winced. 'That's horrible.'

'And it's another lie. My great-great-grandfather knocked her up then denied it. When she threatened to tell people in the village the truth, he pushed her down the stairs.'

Heather fell back into her seat. 'How can you be sure?'

'Because my father used to threaten to do it if Ross ever knocked up any girl out of wedlock.'

'Like me.'

Oh, God. Every generation of Bryce men, Cal had said. But not him. Whatever he thought. He wouldn't do anything to hurt her. She was sure of it.

Cal looked up at her, a wicked glint in his eye. 'You still sure about staying?'

'You wouldn't hurt me,' she said, meeting his gaze head-on, making sure her voice never wavered.

She was rewarded by a sudden vulnerability in his expression. 'How can you *know* that, Heather? How can you know I'm not just like all the rest of them?'

'Because you asked me here tonight to teach you how to love your niece and nephew,' she said softly. 'You're a good man. I don't know what else your father did—or your grandfather and your great-grandfather and so on—to make you think otherwise. But I've only been here two days and I can already see that. So how about you try forgetting about the past and focussing on the future for a change?'

'Like you are?' he asked, his defences back up. 'I know the money I offered you was good, but can you *really* tell me that's the only reason you're staying? That you're not avoiding having to admit to your scandalous pregnancy in your home town?'

Heather looked away. 'I never said that wasn't part of it. My dad doesn't deserve another scandal being brought down on him.'

'And neither do you.'

Reaching between them, Cal took her hand in his, and Heather glanced up to meet his gaze again. The wicked gleam was gone, and so was the anger and the defensiveness. In its place was an expression Heather couldn't quite identify, but it made her stomach flip-flop all the same.

Was ten weeks too early to feel the baby move? Probably. Which meant this was something else.

And whatever it was, it scared her.

'We'll figure this out, okay? Together.' Cal's

voice was rough, as if admitting to his family's past had torn his throat raw.

'Okay,' she whispered back. 'Okay.'

Because she believed him. Even if she had no idea how they could do it.

CHAPTER NINE

CAL WAS SUDDENLY all too aware of the soft-ness of Heather's skin under his fingers and the trusting look in her eyes. God help her, she honestly believed that he was different. That he wasn't just like all the others.

He almost didn't want her to stay long enough to realise she was wrong.

Her copper curls fell around her shoulders and he longed to run his fingers through them. Wanted to reach an arm around her and pull her closer. To brush his hands down her sides, her curves, until they rested at her waist and he could lean in for the inevitable kiss he could feel building...

Except he couldn't.

He could see it in her eyes that if he pressed his lips to hers right now Heather wouldn't pull away. Knew in his bones that she wanted this as much as he did.

Was it the strange closeness that came from knowing each other's secrets? From being with the only other person in the world who knew everything? Or was it something more basic? Primal? A connection between them that came from attraction and lust and nothing more?

Or was it the strange sense of trust she brought out in him—something Cal had thought bred out of him generations ago?

Perhaps the problem was that it was all three. He wanted Heather—but she was beautiful, so that was hardly a surprise. And he could relax with her in a way he couldn't with anyone else, because she knew the truth. Most of all, he trusted her, and that felt wonderful.

But, despite all that, he couldn't have her. Couldn't let himself give in to this moment, however tempting it was.

He might be a Bryce, but Heather had given him a glimmer of hope that he could beat down those genes and actually behave the way the rest of his family pretended they did. She was pregnant with his brother's child. She was scandal enough already—he couldn't make it worse by seducing her.

Especially now he knew what that kind of scandal would do to her, and to her family, if she had to live through it again.

Swallowing hard, Cal pulled back and watched the light in Heather's eyes flicker and fade. But then she gave a small nod and he knew that she understood.

However much they both wanted this, it could never be a good idea. And they were just going to have to live with that.

'I should get back to the children. Check they're actually asleep this time.' Heather was on her feet before she'd finished the sentence. 'Oh, I got in touch with the hospital, by the way. I have a scan booked in two weeks' time.'

'I'll take you,' Cal said automatically.

Heather shook her head. 'You don't need to do that. If you could look after the children while I go, though...'

'Mrs Peterson will take care of them,' Cal insisted. 'You shouldn't be alone for that.'

Whatever else there could or couldn't be between them, Cal knew that going to the scan with Heather was the right thing to do. And Heather always did the right thing for other people. It was time other people started doing the same for her.

'Okay, then,' she said, giving in with a small smile.

'Okay.' He returned it, and their gazes met, and suddenly Cal realised that whole minutes might have passed and he wouldn't have known. He was too lost in her green, green eyes.

That was when he realised he might be in real trouble this time. Some things were just too tempting to resist.

The next few days, after the kiss that never happened, were somehow both awkward and not.

Heather found herself overthinking every tiny interaction she had with Cal. Like the day she stopped by his study with a new book for his reading list that had been delivered, and found him with his head in his hands at the desk. She'd paused in the doorway, uncertain as to whether she should go in, but then he'd looked up, smiled tiredly at her and held out his hand.

What had made her take it, she still didn't

know. Knowing Cal, he wouldn't have offered it if he hadn't been so exhausted. But she knew he'd been working long mornings, from the early hours, spending the afternoons with the children after their lessons had finished, and then working again after dinner before heading down to the small sitting room by the kitchen for kid tuition with her before bed.

No wonder he was worn out.

She'd taken his hand and he'd pulled her close, resting his head against her stomach as she stood beside him. And for a moment—just a blink of a second—she had almost believed that it was his baby growing inside her. That they really were in this together, not just muddling through as partners because they had no other choice.

He'd come to his senses pretty quickly, letting her go so fast that she stumbled backwards.

'I'm sorry,' he'd said, but she'd shaken her head.

She wasn't sorry. But she knew they couldn't have anything more than those stolen moments, either.

She'd placed the book on his desk and left.

But most of the time when they were together the children were there, too—walking in the woods, down by the river, or popping into the village to visit the sweet shop. Cal had relaxed a lot around them, which had helped the kids to relax in turn. Heather couldn't help but think that his lessons in children really were paying off.

Even if the lessons themselves were a torment.

Every night they met in that damn sitting room and talked about Daisy and Ryan—how they were getting on with their lessons, how they could both support them, the counsellors Cal had found for them to talk to about their parents' deaths. They discussed techniques for discipline and support, ways to make important days feel special, what to do when Daisy had another one of her nightmares…

They talked about everything, as long as it had to do with the children.

They never talked again about the secrets they'd shared in that room. Or how sure Heather had been that Cal would have kissed her that night if the circumstances had been different. If she hadn't been pregnant with Ross's child.

And still, underneath all their carefully neutral talk, she could hear echoes of it. In the tone of his voice, or in the smallest aside about her appearance or behaviour.

The connection she'd felt that night hadn't gone away, Heather knew. It just simmered under the surface. And that was where they needed to keep it.

So Heather made sure they both always stayed in their chairs during their lessons, across the room from each other. She tried not to let their fingers touch when she passed him a book or a paper. She tried not to meet his gaze when she smiled. Because then she'd have to watch his eyes turn darker and know it was lust she saw.

Some nights she was more successful than others.

'I think it's time for you to take the kids out on your own,' Heather said, looking up from her notebook to see Cal balancing an apple on his head. Where had he even got the apple *from*?

It rolled off and he caught it as he stared at

her in alarm. 'On my own? I do that all the time. We went into Lengroth last week.'

'Once,' Heather pointed out. 'And I was thinking somewhere a little further afield.'

'But *why*?' Cal whined, sounding so like his nephew that Heather couldn't help but smile.

'Because that's what we're building up to here, right? You being able to look after them alone after I leave.'

A shadow fell across Cal's face. Heather knew her own smile had slipped, too. She didn't like to think about leaving Lengroth Castle, and not only because it meant that Daisy and Ryan would be heading off to boarding school.

Unless I can convince Cal otherwise.

'But you're still here right now,' Cal argued. 'And I'm still learning, right?'

Heather eyed the apple in his hand disapprovingly. 'Yeah, right. *Lots* of learning going on here tonight. Besides, all the education in the world counts for nothing if you can't put it into practice.'

'I thought I was,' Cal grumbled.

Heather took pity on him. 'Yes, you have been.'

In fact, he'd been doing so well she wasn't sure he'd even noticed that she stepped back from any sort of discipline or emotional management of the kids when he was in the room. He might not realise it, but he was doing everything he needed to already. He just needed to take the next step, and continue it when she wasn't there as a safety net.

'That's why we're taking it up a level.'

'Where would I even take them?' he asked.

Heather shrugged. 'Anywhere. Take them bowling, or to the cinema. Crazy golf. Swimming. Soft play.'

Cal pulled a face. 'I've got a meeting with my lawyer in Edinburgh the day after tomorrow—'

'I was thinking more of something that would be fun for *them*,' Heather interrupted.

Cal rolled his eyes. 'I know that. I was thinking the three of you could come with me for the day. The kids could stay with you while I have my meeting, then I could take them around the city on my own afterwards. We could all meet up for dinner before driving back.'

Heather blinked. 'That's actually a really good idea.'

'Then it's a date,' Cal said with a smirk—one that faded quickly when Heather winced. 'Yeah. Not that. You know what I mean…'

'I know,' Heather said.

She also knew that it was moments like that which were going to drive her insane with the effort of not kissing Cal Bryce.

Cal was starting to think that this was a very bad idea.

Edinburgh was packed with tourists—all in town for the Fringe Festival, he supposed. His meeting with the lawyer had gone even more badly than he'd expected. Heather had skipped off for an afternoon in the city alone *after* feeding the kids ice cream and waffles, so he'd have nothing to bribe them with later unless he wanted them on some sort of almighty sugar high. And it was raining.

None of these things were making his mood any brighter.

'So, what do you want to do?' he asked Daisy and Ryan, as they sheltered in a shop doorway, with the sound of bagpipes blasting through the weather on the Royal Mile.

Daisy shrugged. Ryan widened his eyes and shook his head.

'Really helpful, kids.'

'Well, we don't know what there is *to* do,' Daisy pointed out. 'Whenever we came here with Mum it was to go shopping.'

'We don't want to go shopping,' Ryan clarified quickly.

'Good.' Cal rubbed a hand across his forehead as he tried to think about what *he'd* liked about the city as a child. Being away from Lengroth, mostly.

Then he had a stroke of genius.

'Okay. Follow me, stay close and don't wander off.'

He strode through the rain towards Castle Hill and the hulking shadow of Edinburgh Castle, stark against the cloudy sky.

'You *do* realise that we *live* in a castle,' Daisy pointed out as they got closer. 'You really don't need to take us to another one.'

'But what if this one has functioning dungeons?' Cal asked. Beside him, Ryan gasped, and Cal shook his head. 'We're not going to the castle. Come on.'

They stopped at a building just before the castle and Cal hurried his charges inside, out of the rain.

'World of Illusions?' Daisy asked, sticking her head back outside to check the sign.

'What's a Camera Obscura?' Ryan frowned as he sounded out the word on the leaflets by the door.

'Let's head in and find out.'

In his head Cal had imagined introducing the kids to all the different mirror tricks and plasma balls, the mind-bending illusions, and explaining how they worked. The kids would hang off his every word as he made magic real or demonstrated something properly cool.

As it was, the minute they had their tickets and were through the doors Daisy and Ryan both raced off in different directions, leaving him staring after them dumbly.

He shook his head and prepared to yell.

They're just overexcited.

Great. Now he was hearing Heather's voice in his head.

Ryan raced past him again, so Cal grabbed his sleeve as he passed, held his hand firmly—

despite his admonishments that, at eight, he was far too old to hold hands—and headed out to find Daisy.

'Right. Now, here are the rules,' he told them, as the three of them were reunited beside a mirror that stretched them out into giants.

'Set your expectations,' Heather always said. *'Kids like to know what their limits are, even if they go on to test them.'*

With Heather's gentle voice in his head, he forced himself to keep his tone even and calm, rather than just yelling at them. 'We stick together, okay? We can look at everything in here, for as long as you like, but we do it together. And we finish at the Camera Obscura, okay?'

'I still don't know what one of those is,' Ryan grumbled.

'Then let's get exploring,' Cal said, deciding to take their lack of answer as tacit acceptance.

Daisy rolled her eyes, but followed anyway.

To start with, Cal used the kids' fascination with the illusions, the shadow wall and the plasma globes as an opportunity to check his emails. Daisy rolled her eyes at him again, but she and Ryan seemed to be having a nice time so he didn't worry.

When they reached the Ames Room—where an optical illusion meant people appeared to shrink and grow as they moved around—he surrendered his phone to Daisy, so she could take photos of Ryan seemingly much taller than him. Then they reached Bewilderworld, where Cal just concentrated on not feeling dizzy and disorientated as they crossed a metal bridge surrounded by a tunnel of twisting, turning lights.

'Where's Ryan?' he asked Daisy as he stepped off the other end.

'He ran into the mirror maze,' Daisy replied with a shrug. 'I'll go find him.'

She raced off before Cal could stop her. Uncomfortably, he stared into the walls and walls of mirrors and steeled himself to follow.

Apart from flashes of the kids as they ran ahead, their laughter echoing off the glass, all Cal could see was himself, reflected everywhere. A reminder of who he was…who he'd always be. A Bryce, with all the history that brought with it. And, try as he might, he couldn't catch up with Daisy and Ryan, who always seemed just a stretch out of reach.

'This is every parent's worst nightmare,' Cal muttered, before stopping inches away from crashing into another mirror.

Parent. He was the parent—or as close to one as these kids had. And while he might still have a long way to go in learning to take care of them…let alone loving them the way they needed…he was making progress. He was here, in a damn maze, not waiting outside on his phone.

He was here. And that was the first step.

Smiling to himself, he turned confidently left—and walked straight into another mirror pane.

'This way, Uncle Cal!'

He spun to find Ryan waiting behind him.

'Come on!'

This time his nephew grabbed *his* hand and led the way. And Cal couldn't help but admit that it felt strangely right.

CHAPTER TEN

'AND THEN UP in the roof there's this magic camera that lets you see all the streets of Edinburgh right as they're happening, only tiny. And we looked for you but we couldn't see you. But the guy doing the show built a bridge for some other people and they walked right across it and it was brilliant!'

Ryan's epic run-on sentence came to an end and he took a large gulp of the brightly coloured drink he'd ordered from the kids' menu in the restaurant Cal had chosen. Heather was now regretting agreeing to let them have anything they wanted. The E-numbers would keep them awake for a week.

'Magic camera?' she asked Cal, while Ryan was quiet.

'The Camera Obscura,' Cal explained. 'Victorian ingenuity at its finest. Have you ever been?'

Heather shook her head. 'I'll have to go some time.'

Cal opened his mouth—almost as if he were about to say *I'll take you*—then shut it again, so hard she heard his teeth click.

'So you had a good afternoon, then?' she asked, turning to Daisy.

Daisy shrugged. 'It was okay, I suppose.'

Heather gave Cal a small smile. From Daisy, that was high praise indeed. She'd *known* letting them spend the afternoon together was a good idea—and she'd managed to do some much-needed clothes shopping, too. Ordering online could only get a girl so far, especially when it came to maternity bras.

Later, as they drove home into the darkening summer sky, with Ryan passed out in the back and Daisy with her headphones on, Heather asked, 'Was it really a good afternoon?'

Cal's smile was slow, but telling. 'You know…it was. I mean, there's a big difference between a few hours at a tourist attraction and the rest of their lives, but it was good. It's a start, right?'

'A really good one,' Heather said, and tried to ignore the warmth that filled her at his words.

She was *not* falling for her boss. And she was *definitely* not falling for the brother of her baby's father. No matter how gorgeous he was when he smiled. Not happening.

She hoped.

'Daisy did well on her history assignment this week,' Heather said, handing Cal a printout of Daisy's short essay as they sat in the little sitting room by the kitchen a few days later.

Despite Cal's progress he'd insisted on continuing their kid lessons, even if they were mostly just catch-ups on how they'd got on that day.

'Seems she has a real grasp of the blood and guts part of historical conflict.'

'Why am I not surprised?' Cal took it, grinning up at her, and Heather knew it was pride she saw in his gaze.

She couldn't help it; she smiled back. Just as their fingers touched and his eyes turned dark again…

Was this how her mother had felt? Falling for

someone she knew she couldn't have? She'd been married, he'd been thirteen years younger than her... Her mother couldn't have thought it was a good idea.

And yet she'd fallen for him anyway. Been so consumed by love and lust that she'd left her whole life behind for him.

Heather, fortunately, wasn't that stupid.

She might not be able to stop the feelings that flooded through her every time she was with Cal, but she could call them what they were. Attraction. Lust. And wildly inappropriate.

She pulled back quickly and turned her attention to her notes. She'd found early on that if she didn't approach each evening with a list of things to discuss with Cal about the children it was too easy to forget everything she'd meant to say when she was with him. Or for the conversation to get distracted, to stray onto forbidden topics.

Like how badly she wanted to kiss him.

It hadn't felt like this with Ross, she realised. Or anyone else ever, actually. This incredible drawn-out anticipation of something that couldn't happen.

With Ross, it had been a stupid idea after one too many cocktails. He'd been gorgeous, oozing confidence, and she'd been having a bad day. He'd wanted her, and she'd wanted cheering up, and that had been enough.

But with Cal... *Want* wasn't a strong enough word to encompass the feeling that flooded through her every time she saw him. It seemed impossible that they'd never even kissed. That her body could hum with need just being in the same room as him, yet she'd never felt his lips on hers or his hands against her bare skin.

And it felt even more impossible that she never would.

'How about Ryan?' Cal asked, clearing his throat first.

Heather forced herself back into the moment. 'Um...he's doing fine, too. A little distracted this week, actually. I'm not sure why.'

Cal shrugged, as if to say *Why are you asking me?* Heather was about to remind him exactly why this was his problem, too, when his face fell and his eyes grew wide.

'Oh, hell.'

'What?'

'It's his birthday. This weekend.'

Cal looked mortified that he'd forgotten. Heather was just relieved that he'd remembered *now*.

'I need to buy him a present, right? What on earth do I get him?'

Of course he thought this was all about the present. Ryan's first birthday without his parents there to celebrate with him and Cal thought it could be fixed with a remote-control helicopter or something.

Which actually wasn't a bad gift idea, now she thought about it. But it wasn't going to be enough.

Chewing on her lower lip, Heather doodled a helicopter on the notepad in front of her.

'Actually,' she said slowly, 'I've got a good idea.'

Cal wasn't entirely sure how him organising Ryan's birthday celebrations was a *good* idea. In fact, it seemed like a bad one to him. But Heather was adamant.

'It's the perfect opportunity for you to show

him that you're here, that he's not parentless, and that you know important things about him.'

'Like when his birthday is?'

'Like what he enjoys and how he'd like to celebrate,' Heather corrected him.

Cal sighed. 'Except that's the point. I *don't* know that stuff.'

'Well, if his birthday is on Saturday you've got three days to learn. Right? And you did okay in Edinburgh. You'll be fine.'

Not helpful. If he'd remembered that Ryan's birthday was coming up he'd definitely have saved the trip to the World of Illusions for that. Now he was all out of ideas.

As if he didn't have enough to do without a nine-year-old's birthday party to arrange. He'd tried quizzing Daisy on what sort of things they'd done for birthdays before, but that hadn't been as helpful as he'd hoped.

'Mostly we just had a birthday tea here,' she'd said with a shrug. 'Mum would get a cake from the bakery in town, and sometimes we'd invite a friend each, but that was about it.'

Well, cake he could manage. Friends he could not. As far as he'd seen since he'd returned neither child had any—or wanted any. They were happiest in each other's company.

Although, as a book on Heather's reading list had informed him, that was probably because they were the only people who understood what they'd each been through.

A bit like him and Heather, really. They'd both been disillusioned by someone they loved, and both had had to cope with a scandal looming over their heads, waiting to break.

And he absolutely wasn't going to make it worse by kissing her. However much he wanted to. God, he really wanted to.

Except when she landed him with things like organising Ryan's party.

In the end he'd come up with a plan, of sorts—only slightly assisted by Heather on the subject of present ideas. He had no idea if Ryan would have chosen the same things to celebrate turning nine, but at least it showed he was making an effort—he hoped.

This stuff he could do. This kind of thing came with an action list and a basic template. He could follow instructions well enough. It was figuring out how to deal with the stuff that *didn't* come with a manual—like emotions and love—that caused him problems.

Saturday dawned sunny and bright, fortunately for Cal's plans. Mrs Peterson made pancakes for breakfast—much to everyone's delight—and Ryan opened presents from Daisy, Heather, Mrs Peterson and Cal himself.

Heather's presents were books, unsurprisingly, but since they seemed to be about some sort of monsters, and brave young boys capturing and training them, Ryan was thrilled. Daisy had spent some of her pocket money in the sweet shop last time they went to the village, so Ryan now had enough sugary chewy things to rot his teeth for months. Mrs Peterson had bought him a sensible jumper for the Scottish winters. And Cal, on Heather's advice, had bought him a remote-control helicopter.

'This is awesome! Thank you, Uncle Cal!'

Cal shot a grateful smile at Heather. 'I'm glad you like it. How about we take it out for the day and see how it flies?'

'All day?' Ryan asked. 'No lessons first?'

'No lessons on birthdays,' Heather confirmed. 'It's a rule.'

'For me, too?' Daisy asked.

'Absolutely,' Cal told her. 'Go on, you two— go and get ready to head out. We'll meet you at the front door in twenty minutes.'

'So far so good,' Heather murmured as the kids raced off.

'Long way to go yet,' Cal replied.

This was going well. Against all the odds— and definitely all his expectations—this was going well.

Cal had spent some time thinking about when he'd seen Ryan look happiest, or most relaxed, and had realised that it was whenever they were outside. Ryan was all boy, after all, and constantly moving, so getting him somewhere he could run and jump and yell just made sense.

Especially since they could also fly the new helicopter.

'I swear you're more excited about that thing than he is,' Heather had muttered as Cal and Ryan had planned flights and adventures for it on the drive there.

He'd chosen an area he and Ross had loved exploring as kids, whenever they'd been able to persuade someone to take them. Just past Lengroth Woods, at the edge of their estate, was a valley with a stream running through it, steep hills for rolling down on either side, purple heather and yellow gorse blooming all around, and no people for miles in any direction.

It was perfect for a family walk, a picnic in the sunshine—and for sending the helicopter on its first mission, to find out how good the inbuilt camera that was meant to talk to his smartphone really was.

Pretty good, was the answer. As they all settled down for their birthday lunch Cal and Ryan reviewed the footage together, heads close as they stared at the little screen.

Something tightened in Cal's chest as Ryan's hair brushed against his cheek, and he realised that maybe—*maybe*—this was what he'd been looking for. A connection with these children he didn't know and couldn't understand. There hadn't even been the tension between them that he'd felt in Edinburgh, when they'd still been figuring out how to spend time together at all.

Maybe all those lessons with Heather were paying off.

He looked up, wanting to share the moment with her, only to find her already watching him, with the softest of smiles on her face. She already knew, he realised as he returned the smile.

'Is it time for cake now?' Daisy asked, sounding bored. 'I only really came for the cake.'

Heather rolled her eyes. 'Of course you did. Hang on.'

She pulled a large bakery box from the picnic basket they'd lugged from the car, fiddled around with some candles and matches, then presented it to Ryan as they all chorused a slightly off-key version of 'Happy Birthday'.

Ryan beamed as he bent forward to blow out the candles, and Cal snapped a photo on his phone so he could remember this moment. The day when he'd finally started getting something right.

He just hoped he could keep it up.

* * *

Heather thought her heart might burst as she watched Cal and Ryan together as they flew the helicopter back down the valley to the four-by-four.

She and Daisy were walking behind, a little slower, enjoying the last of the sweet summer air blowing off the stream. Even in August it grew a little chilly as the sun started to sink, and they'd stayed much longer than they'd intended since they were having such a lovely day.

Heather couldn't remember the last time she'd lazed around in the sunshine like that. She and Cal had sat in companionable silence as the kids had raced around collecting flowers from the heather and gorse, or paddling in the stream as far as they could go before the current got too strong. For once the tension between them seemed to have faded, and they'd just been able to enjoy the day.

Heather hadn't felt so relaxed, happy and at home since she'd arrived in Lengroth.

'Did you tell him to do all that?' Daisy asked

suddenly, and in an instant Heather's shoulders tensed again. 'All the birthday stuff, I mean.'

'Actually, no,' Heather replied honestly. 'He remembered it was Ryan's birthday, and I suggested he did something special, but the actual plan was all his.'

'He asked me about the cake.' Daisy sounded faintly horrified that she might have aided and abetted the plan.

'He wanted to get it right. For Ryan.'

'Why?' Daisy sounded honestly confused by her uncle's efforts. 'He never cared about us before Mum and Dad died—we barely saw him except at Christmas, and not always even then.'

'Things are different now.'

'Like I don't *know* that,' Daisy huffed.

Heather tried to find a different tack. 'He's your guardian now,' she said gently. 'He might not know how to be that just yet, but I reckon nobody does when they start. I mean, think about your parents. They were just handed you one day, and suddenly they were responsible for a whole human being. That's got to be kind of scary.'

'They had nine months to get ready for me,'

Daisy said sceptically. 'I *do* know how pregnancy works, you realise.'

Heather noticed almost too late that she had one hand clutched around her middle, as if she were protecting her secret. She tried to drop her arm casually and hoped Daisy didn't know as much as she thought she did. Until she'd had her twelve-week scan she and Cal had agreed it was better not to tell the children she was pregnant.

How they were going to tell them *after* that was a whole different question they hadn't answered yet.

'Even with preparation time it's a huge undertaking, and I don't think it's one you can really prepare for,' Heather went on, feeling the truth of her words in the weight on her shoulders.

She *definitely* wasn't going to be prepared in six months' time. Right now she didn't even know where she would be living.

'I suppose Uncle Cal didn't have those nine months...' Daisy said thoughtfully.

'Exactly!'

'So this summer...this is sort of like Uncle Cal's pregnancy,' Daisy went on. 'I mean, he's figuring out how to look after us and you're helping him, right?'

'Right. At least, I'm trying to.'

Daisy didn't look at her as she answered. 'I don't think you're doing *too* badly. At least not as bad as some of the others.'

Then she raced forward to catch up to Cal and Ryan without even glancing back.

Heather stopped by the edge of the stream, watching after her, as Daisy swung on Cal's arm and made him drop the picnic basket. She waited, tense, for Cal to complain, or even shout—but instead she heard his laughter, echoing back through the valley.

Ryan had had a good birthday. Daisy had opened up to her a bit. And Cal had laughed.

Maybe she *wasn't* doing too badly after all.

Now she just needed to figure out how to fix things for herself and her own baby before it arrived. Starting with Wednesday's scan.

Heather followed the others towards the setting sun and the car, and hoped that things were on the right track now.

They were all due a little bit of luck, she reckoned.

CHAPTER ELEVEN

TRAFFIC WAS BAD driving into Edinburgh on Wednesday morning. Cal wished he'd put the radio on or something when they'd set out—anything to distract them both from the awkward silence and the thought of what was ahead. But they were nearly at the hospital now, and putting it on at this point would only draw more attention to the awkwardness.

'Are you okay?' Heather asked from the passenger seat, a small line forming between her copper brows.

'I'm pretty sure I'm supposed to be the one asking *you* that,' he pointed out. 'You're the one with a hospital appointment in twenty minutes.'

'It's a scan. I'm not scared.'

Cal shot her a disbelieving look. He could hear the nerves in her voice.

'Much,' she amended, obviously reluctantly. 'I just don't want to be late.'

'We won't be,' Cal promised, silently cursing the traffic ahead.

In the end, they almost were.

Cal wheeled into the hospital approach, a little faster than was probably advisable, and reached across her to open the passenger door. 'Go on. You go in and get registered. I'll park up and meet you in there.'

She nodded, straightened her shoulders and got out of the car.

Cal sped off, risked parking his car somewhere it was almost certainly going to get scraped by passing traffic, because it was the only place left, then raced back to the hospital entrance, spinning through the revolving doors so fast he was half-afraid he'd end up going round twice.

'Whoa!' A man in a nurse's uniform caught him by the shoulder as he stumbled out. 'What's the rush, mate? *Cal?*'

Cal took a hurried step back, scanning the man's face as he tried to place him. 'Harry?'

Harry Malcolm—a classmate from Lengroth Primary, before Cal's father had pulled him out and sent him away to boarding school. His fa-

ther was the postman in Lengroth, his grandmother the biggest gossip in the whole village.
There wasn't anything Enid Malcolm didn't
know about what went on in Lengroth.

Including, after this, the news that Cal Bryce
had been seen at the hospital in Edinburgh with
his nanny. *Perfect.*

Harry beamed. 'That's right! I wasn't sure
if you'd remember. My nan says you're practically the Earl up at Lengroth these days. We
were all surprised that you'd come back, last
time I was down the pub with the old crowd.'

'I'm not the Earl,' Cal corrected him, scanning the lobby for any sign of Heather. Maybe
she'd already gone through to wherever it was
she was supposed to go. He'd have to ask. Ask
anyone except Harry, that was. 'Ryan is. I'm
just his guardian.'

'Yeah, but you're responsible for everything
that happens up there, right?'

'Unfortunately.' Suddenly Cal spotted a head
of copper curls headed their way.

Heather. *Damn.* He'd never thought he'd be
unhappy to see her.

He shot her a look across the lobby and she

frowned. Resisting the urge to roll his eyes, he jerked his head away from Harry and hoped she'd got the message.

The last thing he needed to do right now was explain to Harry—and by extension to Harry's grandmother and the rest of Lengroth—why he was visiting the maternity unit with his niece and nephew's nanny.

'Look—sorry, mate—but I've got to…' Cal pointed vaguely in the direction of a corridor that he hoped didn't lead to anything embarrassing.

'Sure…right. Well, good to see you!' Harry clapped Cal on the shoulder and wandered off—right past an annoyed-looking Heather.

'Sorry about that.' Cal hurried over to her the moment Harry was gone. 'But, trust me, we did *not* want to be seen here together by him.'

'Right. Whatever… Come on—we're going to be late. It's this way.'

Heather moved away with long strides down another corridor—one with paintings on the wall and motivational quotes in swirly fonts. Cal ignored them and kept his eyes on the copper hair in front of him and the swing of her hips.

She was angry. He could tell that much by the way her hair snaked from side to side as she walked and the force of her step. He could read her body so easily, considering he'd never even touched it.

What he *couldn't* quite figure out, however, was why. Heather wanted to avoid a scandal as much as he did—so she couldn't possibly object to him taking steps to do that, could she?

She'd tell him in her own time, he supposed. And in the meantime they had a scan to get to.

Cal quickened his step to catch her up.

She shouldn't be annoyed. Heather *knew* she shouldn't be annoyed.

But she was.

However unforeseen the circumstances, she was here for the first scan of her first child—maybe her only child. She was going to see her baby inside her. It was a special, momentous day.

Was it too much to ask for it just to be treated normally—not hidden away and treated as an embarrassment?

Apparently so.

Heather sighed. She knew what Cal had been trying to do. He'd explained about Harry and Harry's grandmother once she'd checked in with Reception and they had been sent to sit in the waiting area. It all made perfect sense—after all, she *didn't* want the whole of Lengroth talking about her and Cal, especially since there *was* no 'her and Cal'.

But another, nagging part of her brain kept reminding her that it was the secrecy and the lies that had been the worst when the truth had come out about her mother's affair. And the lies she'd told after that—the ones that had given her dad hope again and made him defend her mother to strangers. It was the broken trust that had been the hardest thing to fix.

Cal's family had spent generations pretending to be perfect, while behind closed doors they'd behaved however they'd pleased, whomever it had hurt. Was she wrong to be worried that Cal was just carrying on the tradition he'd claimed to hate?

'When are we going to tell Daisy and Ryan?' she asked suddenly, as another couple were led into the scanning room.

Beside her, Cal started, looking up from the *Mother and Baby* magazine he was flicking through.

'Uh… I don't know. I guess it depends what you want to happen in September.'

Of course. By September—just a few weeks away now—she'd be gone from Lengroth. If she didn't want to she'd never have to see Cal or the kids again. They'd never know about their half-brother or sister. She knew for certain that Cal would never tell them if she chose to go.

Nobody would know. The scandal would be contained. Sure, she'd still be an unwed mother, but that was nothing these days. She could even claim she'd chosen it—gone to a sperm bank and picked a donor. One with dark hair and amber eyes.

She could tell whatever lies she wanted. But she knew the truth always came out in the end.

'I want Daisy and Ryan to be part of their half-brother or half-sister's life,' she said firmly. 'And that means telling them the truth.'

How that would work back home in Hertfordshire… Well, maybe it was time to move on, anyway. Move away from home and out of the shadow of her mother's scandal. Her father was doing so well these days—she was sure he'd be fine.

Of course, telling Daisy and Ryan also meant that Cal would be a part of her life, Heather realised. For ever.

She wasn't entirely sure how she felt about that. Half of her was cheering, because she couldn't imagine *not* having him around. The rest of her was wondering how on earth they'd manage it without falling into bed eventually.

But maybe—just maybe—that would be okay. Maybe eventually the risk of scandal would pass and nobody would care. They just had to wait it out.

'I don't want to rush it,' Cal said finally. 'They've been through so much and we're finally making progress. They're relaxing, opening up to me and letting me in. And Daisy hasn't thrown anything out of the window at people in weeks—not since that stupid rubber duck you carried in on your first day.'

Heather smiled at the memory. When she'd seen that duck bobbing along in the moat she'd had no idea where it would lead her.

'I guess I just don't want to ruin all our hard work, right before they leave for school,' Cal said, with a sigh.

'You're still planning on sending them away, then?' Heather asked.

Cal looked at her, surprised. 'Of course. It's the best thing for their education.'

'Right...' But was it the best thing for their lives? Just when she'd thought Cal was making real progress...

'Heather Reid?' a nurse called, and they both stood up.

'Ready for this?' Cal asked, and Heather nodded.

'I think so.'

Suddenly he grabbed her hand. 'Heather... I really am so sorry my brother dragged you into all this. I know this can't be how you dreamed about doing this, with *me* here at your side. But I *am* here, for whatever you need.'

'I know.'

Heather smiled gently as she realised the truth. Maybe this wasn't what she'd planned for her life, and it wasn't what she'd have chosen if she'd been given a choice. But she'd have been wrong.

Because right now there was no one else she wanted with her except Cal. And that terrified her almost as much as the prospect of becoming a mother did.

'Come on. Let's go see this baby.'

'Now, Daddy, if you'd like to come and sit on this side, please?' the technician asked, oblivious to the confusion she'd thrown up inside Cal.

He glanced over at Heather, settling herself on the table and lifting her top to show off smooth white skin. He looked away quickly.

Should he correct the technician? Explain that he wasn't the father, but the uncle. And her employer. Maybe friend…?

But it was too late already. The moment had passed. And besides, surely that would only make a bigger deal of everything? Make them more memorable if someone asked, later, if he'd gone in. Not that they would. Probably.

You never knew with Lengroth people. They were the worst gossips in the world. It was a minor miracle that the Bryce family had never been rumbled before, quite honestly. Or perhaps that was how they'd got so good at hiding the truth.

Maybe he was just discombobulated because of their conversation in the waiting room, Cal decided as he took the indicated seat at last. He'd imagined that come September Heather would walk out of their lives again. That she'd realise she didn't want any part of the Bryce legacy and leave.

The kids would miss her, but they'd be away at school anyway, making new friends, so they'd cope. And he... Well, he hadn't done much thinking about how *he'd* cope without her. Without seeing those bright green eyes every morning, or catching flashes of those coppery curls around the castle.

Hadn't *wanted* to think about it.

But what place was there for her at Lengroth with the children gone? He couldn't very well ask her to stay because he might get lonely. People would talk.

So what if they did?

Cal pushed the errant thought aside. He

couldn't make Heather the centre of a scandal, and he couldn't ruin the reputation of Lengroth and the Bryce family for Daisy and Ryan. It was as simple as that.

However much he wanted to.

But if she wanted to stay in their lives… What would that mean, exactly? Visits at Christmas and birthdays? Emails and postcards?

That wasn't enough for him.

Nothing he could have with Heather would be.

Because he'd realised that the truth was he *wanted* to be here at her side today. Not because she was carrying his brother's child. But because he wanted to be part of her life.

That's just lust talking. The good old Bryce desire for whatever is worst for us.

But he needed to be different for Daisy and Ryan. He couldn't give in to it.

The technician smeared jelly over Heather's still-flat stomach and held the wand. 'Are we ready to see our baby?'

Our baby.

Cal swallowed hard as he nodded, not daring to look at Heather's face. He kept his eyes firmly on the screen as a picture started to emerge. A grainy black-and-white picture of nothing that made any sense until the technician suddenly beamed and said, 'There we are! Right there. Can you see the head?'

And suddenly he could. He could see Heather's baby.

His heart thumped too loud in his chest—so loud he was sure Heather must be able to hear it. The whole *hospital* could probably hear it.

He felt like he had when Ryan had bent his head close to his on his birthday, as he'd climbed into his car seat, and whispered, 'This was a brilliant birthday, Uncle Cal.' Like he had when Daisy had stopped by his office yesterday to ask him a question about her maths homework and then stayed and chatted for twenty minutes about nothing and everything.

He felt like he did late at night, when he walked Heather to her bedroom after their tutoring sessions. Which neither of them would give up even though he wasn't sure they were learning anything new. And sometimes, if she was tired enough, she'd lean her forehead against his chest, just for a moment, and he'd feel her warm breath through his shirt.

He'd never had a name for those feelings—the feelings that thrummed through his veins and told him he was truly alive. He'd known they were important, but just getting to experience them had been enough for him. He hadn't wanted to label them in case it scared them away.

But now…

He twisted round to look at Heather and found her staring at the screen in wonder. Then, as if she'd sensed his gaze on her, she turned to smile at him—and there was a whole world in that smile. A whole future.

Cal let himself drink it in, just for a moment.

Then he swallowed and looked away.

Lust. That was all it was. He wanted her because she was the worst person in the world he should desire and he was a Bryce.

He was the Bryce legacy come true all over again, but he was damned if he was going to give in to it.

CHAPTER TWELVE

SOMETHING ODD WAS going on with Cal. Well, odder than normal, anyway.

Ever since they'd got back from the hospital after the scan he'd been going out of his way to avoid her. Heather couldn't decide if it was because of the guy he'd bumped into in the hospital lobby, the conversation they'd had about telling Daisy and Ryan, or the strange expression she'd seen on his face when the technician had shown them the baby, wriggling around on the screen.

She knew how strange this must be for him. He'd gained two children almost from nowhere and now there was a third on the way. But he had to realise that she wouldn't ask him for anything for *her* baby, right? If he wanted to be part of their little family then she would welcome him. But she was just as prepared to go it alone if she had to, as she had been the day she'd arrived at Lengroth.

No. That wasn't quite true. She wasn't the same person she'd been the day she'd first climbed those steps. That woman was gone for ever, and Heather couldn't quite bring herself to miss her.

That woman had been almost without hope. She'd been weighed down by guilt and fear and desperation. And, while the guilt still lingered, she hoped she'd at least gone some way towards making amends by helping the children this summer. As for the fear... She'd been afraid because she hadn't had faith in herself to fix her situation. Now she knew it didn't need fixing—and she had complete confidence that whatever happened next she would be able to handle it.

Even if that meant being a single mother, ostracised by her father and everyone in her village, and hundreds of miles away from Cal, Daisy and Ryan.

Worst-case scenario, Heather. Don't think about it.

'Where's your uncle?' she asked as she sat down to dinner with the children a few days later.

Daisy shrugged. 'I went to call him. He yelled at me to go away.' She was obviously trying to sound nonchalant, but failing.

Heather had been surprised the first time she'd stopped by Cal's office and heard Daisy's voice behind the door. But now it was every bit as everyday an occurrence as Ryan stealing the last piece of toast at breakfast. Heather couldn't entirely explain it—and she knew for a fact that Cal had no idea how it had happened— but Daisy had not just warmed to Cal, but had latched on to him completely.

They talked about everything, Cal had said, from the planets to the environment, from the history of the castle to West End musicals. And somewhere in all that, when she needed to, Daisy would slip in a comment about something that was bothering her and Cal would try to help her. Or, more often, report it to Heather, who would give him advice so he could tackle it the next day.

As far as Heather could tell, his whole relationship with Daisy had more of a big-brother vibe than a parental one, but if that was what Daisy needed then she was happy she had found it.

Or seemed to have until tonight.

'I'm sure he was just very busy,' Heather said soothingly, even as she exchanged a worried glance with Mrs Peterson.

The housekeeper widened her eyes and shrugged, to indicate that she didn't know what was going on, either.

'Whatever…' Daisy mumbled towards her plate. 'I don't care.'

'Shall I go call him again?' Ryan jumped to his feet before he'd even finished his question.

'You stay here and eat,' Heather said quickly. 'If Uncle Cal is busy he probably won't want to come down for dinner. I'll take him up a plate once we've eaten.'

The meal was a mostly silent one. Afterwards, with the kids settled in their bedrooms after baths and tooth-brushing, Heather took the dinner tray that Mrs Peterson had put together and carried it carefully towards Cal's study, bracing herself for the response she was likely to get.

Balancing the tray on one hip, she knocked lightly.

'I said I'm not coming down for dinner!'

Heather rolled her eyes and inched the door open. 'That's why dinner has come to you.'

Not waiting for an invitation, she crossed the study, placed the tray on the desk in front of him—handily covering whatever papers had him so work-obsessed this evening—then sat in the chair opposite him.

'Heather, I really don't have time—'

'Then *make* time.'

Something in her voice obviously caught his attention because he looked up, rubbing a hand across the back of his neck.

He looked exhausted, Heather realised. Not just tired, but worn thin and on the edge of everything. The fine lines around his eyes were suddenly more pronounced, and the shadows under them were grey and heavy.

'Cal!'

Heather hopped up again and moved around to the other side of the desk, leaning against it so he had to sit back in his chair to look up at her.

Food could wait. This was more important.

'Tell me. What's going on?'

What was going on? Everything—all at the same time. And he couldn't focus on any of it because he kept seeing the soft smile on Heather's face as she'd looked at her scan picture in the car on the way home, or remembering the way she'd hugged him and whispered 'thank you' in his ear afterwards.

As if that wasn't bad enough, he'd started dreaming about her, too. And those dreams were far less chaste than his memories… Everything he wanted and couldn't have.

'Heather… I can't talk about it.'

How could he tell her how much he wanted her *now*—when this damn reporter was arriving next week and his lawyer had told him there wasn't a thing he could do about it unless he wanted to repay a hell of a lot of money and deal with articles in the magazine speculating on why the Bryce family were so secretive about what was going on at Lengroth Castle these days.

That would only lead them to reinvestigating the circumstances of Ross's death, and Cal wasn't sure any of them wanted to know what they might find out.

He definitely didn't. Which was why he hadn't asked any more questions before now.

Heather's fingers smoothed across his forehead, cool to the touch and instantly calming. Cal took a deeper breath and found himself relaxing against all his instincts.

'I think you need to talk about it,' she said softly. 'Because it's eating you up. I think maybe we've both not talked about things for too long.'

Cal looked up and met her bright green gaze and knew she was right. Ignoring things hadn't got either of them very far up until now.

Apparently she saw something in his expression that gave her encouragement, because she shifted closer—so near that if he just reached out and let go he would have her in his arms in a heartbeat.

'Tell me what you're thinking,' Heather whispered, and Cal felt something open up inside him.

Floodgates, perhaps. Or a door in the walls he'd built up to keep his family's secrets inside. For a moment he felt again as if Heather was standing on those stupid seventeen steps up to the castle door, a rubber duck tucked under her arm, knocking on the ancient wood and asking to come inside.

And, just like last time, he let her in.

'I'm thinking that my whole family is a curse.' Seeing her look, he corrected himself. 'Not the children—although who knows? Give them time… They probably don't have any more chance of avoiding the family legacy of scandal than I do.'

'I think you're doing pretty well,' Heather said.

Cal stared up at her incredulously. 'Are you kidding? I'm sitting here trying to cover up all my brother's misdeeds—just like all the Bryce men before me—and pretending they didn't happen, that people weren't hurt, and that we shouldn't have to pay for our mistakes because we have a castle and some money.'

He looked up at her, flinching at the pity in her eyes. Didn't she realise he was doing exactly the same thing to her?

'Look at you,' he murmured, taking her hand. 'I'm hiding you away in this castle, pretending you're not pregnant by my own brother, letting you help raise his orphaned kids and hiding from anyone who might figure out the truth.'

'So this is about the guy you bumped into at the hospital?'

Harry and his gossipy grandmother. Did she honestly think that was all that was eating him alive from the inside?

Cal shook his head. 'It's not about Harry. It's about this damn castle. It's about Daisy and Ryan. And it's about...' He trailed off. He couldn't say it. He couldn't put that on her. She had more than enough to deal with right now, without bringing his inability to control his libido into the mix.

It's only because I can't have her, he reminded himself. The forbidden was always the most alluring to Bryce men.

But Heather slid a little closer and he couldn't bring himself to look away from her gaze. He felt locked in place, staring into those green eyes, searching them for the same truths he held inside himself.

'It's about…?' she asked, so softly it was barely more than a breath.

'It's about the way I don't think I can make it for another moment without kissing you,' he said, before his brain or his sense of shame could talk him out of it.

Heather bit down on her lower lip and his caution jumped out of the castle window and into the moat. In a heartbeat he had her in his arms, her legs swung over his as he pulled her into his lap.

He'd tried. Really he had. He'd tried to be the one good Bryce man, the one male in the family who'd avoided scandal and stayed away from temptation. He'd tried not giving in to it when temptation had come knocking, with a rubber duck tucked under her arm.

But it was no good. Bad blood won out, and he couldn't fight his genes any longer.

So, with a relief so palpable he could feel his

whole body relaxing as the decision was made, Cal kissed Heather, and forgot—just for now— all the reasons that this was the worst idea he'd ever had.

Oh, God, she was kissing Cal Bryce.

The one thing she'd absolutely sworn to herself that she wouldn't do. One of the few things she could do to make her own scandalous situation worse.

And hands down it was the best kiss of her whole damn life.

Heather allowed herself to fall into the kiss, to experience every sensation and luxuriate in them. His hands on her back, firm and warm. His lips against hers, so sure and confident that she had to wonder if he'd been imagining this moment as much as she had.

And the very hard evidence against her hip that told her this wasn't just an accidental or a casual kiss.

He wanted her.

A lot.

And the feeling was very, *very* mutual.

Heather let out a small gasp as Cal deepened

the kiss, pulling her into him until she wasn't sure where she ended and he began. She shifted in his lap, trying to free her arm from where it was trapped between them, desperate to use it to touch him, feel him, make this experience last for ever…

Which was, of course, when she unbalanced them completely.

Cal swore as the chair tipped backwards towards the window, reaching out with both hands to grab the desk and stop them falling. Heather, however, no longer tethered by his arms, tumbled back towards the floor, and he let go of the desk to catch her—resulting in them both tipping sideways off the chair and landing on the Persian rug under his desk.

'This was *not* how I intended this to go.'

Cal let his head fall back onto the floor, and Heather patted his arm sympathetically as she rested her cheek against his chest.

'Maybe we'll do better next time,' she said.

Cal's hand, which had been rubbing slow circles against her side, stilled, and she knew she'd said the wrong thing.

'Heather… I shouldn't have done that. I'm sorry.'

Something cold settled in her heart. 'Shouldn't have tipped me onto the floor of your office or shouldn't have kissed me like that?'

Like it meant *everything.*

'I think *you* tipped us,' Cal pointed out. 'And I shouldn't have kissed you. It was…inappropriate.'

'You mean scandalous.' Heather sat up, brushing her unruly hair away from her eyes as she stared down at him.

'You're pregnant with my brother's child,' Cal reminded her—as if she didn't already know. 'And you're my employee.'

'I hoped I was your friend, too.'

'Friends don't kiss friends like *that*,' Cal said, his eyes shut tight, and she knew he'd felt it, too.

Knew that the kiss had meant as much to him as it had to her.

'Cal…' She stared down at him, willing him to open his eyes and look at her.

As if he'd heard her thoughts, he did. 'Heather. We can't.'

'Why? *Why* can't we?'

Yes, yes, she knew the reasons. Had argued them with herself for weeks now. But in the end it came down to basics. Undeniable, irresistible basics. He wanted her. She wanted him. His brother certainly hadn't had such reservations...

Oh. 'Is this because of Ross?'

'Indirectly.' Cal gave a tired sigh and pushed himself up to a seated position, leaning back against the desk. His dinner would have gone cold by now, Heather thought as she watched him. He'd be hungry later. But this was more important.

'Because I slept with him first?' she pressed.

She hadn't thought that Cal was the sort of guy to judge her for her past behaviour, but she supposed it *was* a kind of unusual situation. She couldn't blame him for finding it confusing—she certainly did.

'No! Not because...' He swallowed so hard she could see his throat move. 'It's just...the situation.'

'Yeah...'

She knew what he meant, she thought. After

all, hadn't she been stamping down her feelings for Cal for weeks now, for exactly the same reason? All this could lead to was scandal and gossip and talk. The situation was so far from ideal it was laughable. Who got pregnant by an earl who inconveniently died and then fell in love with his brother?

Except…

'Except if it wasn't for this situation I never would have met you,' she said, and the hope in Cal's eyes gave her all the courage she needed to go on. 'Do you think I haven't regretted that night in the bar a million times?' she asked. 'When I found out Ross was married I was physically sick—did I tell you that? I've spent my whole life trying to avoid a situation like this—well, not exactly like this, because I never even imagined that *this* was an option for someone like me—but avoiding scandal and talk. I've tried *so hard* to do the right thing—always. For my dad, yes, but for me, too. Because it *mattered* to me. And then I let my guard down for one night and—'

She broke off, shook her head and started again.

'The point is—yes, I made mistakes. And, yes, I regret them—in a way. Except not completely. Not any more.'

'Why?' Cal's voice was dry and cracked, as if he wasn't sure he could take the answer but felt compelled to ask the question anyway.

'Because if I hadn't met Ross that night I wouldn't have my baby growing inside me right now—a baby that I already love so much. If I hadn't come here to Lengroth to find Ross I'd never have met Daisy and Ryan, whom I adore. And...'

Could she say it? She had to, Heather knew. This had been building for too long, drawing them together while forcing them apart all at the same time.

'And I never would have met you,' she said.

CHAPTER THIRTEEN

CAL STARED UP at Heather's beautiful face, trying to imagine a world in which he didn't know her. Didn't want her.

He couldn't.

If she was just beautiful, or sexy, that would be one thing. He could resist that kind of charm when he wanted to—which, to be honest, wasn't all that often. Under these circumstances, it would be easy.

But Heather was more than that. She'd worked her way into his life—and into the castle—so deeply that he couldn't imagine her not being there. She was his *friend*, as well as the most desirable woman he'd ever met. She was good and kind and all the things that Lengroth Castle normally killed.

Daisy and Ryan needed her in their lives. Which meant he couldn't wreck this by giving in to his lust. Except it wasn't just *his* lust they were dealing with here, apparently.

'What is it?'

His face must have given him away, because in a moment she was sitting back down beside him, her expression concerned.

'Heather… I need you to not take this the wrong way.'

'Suggesting that there is a *very* wrong way for me to take it?' Heather said.

Cal resisted the urge to wince. 'Yeah, you might.'

Heather folded her arms across her chest. Cal forced himself not to stare at the neckline of her summer dress, or the wonderful things the action was doing for her breasts.

Are they always that perfectly plump? Or is it the pregnancy?

Maybe he would find out one day. But not until after this damn summer was over.

'I'm listening,' she said, and Cal tried to find his train of thought again.

'As much as I loved kissing you—and, trust me, I really did—we can't do it again.' It was as simple and frustrating as that.

'Because I'm a scandal for sleeping with your brother and getting pregnant or because your family is cursed?'

She didn't seem to be taking this very seriously, Cal noticed. And he was almost certain she was pushing her breasts up on purpose. To torment him.

It was totally working.

Until he remembered the real reason they couldn't do this.

'Both. But also because Ross signed a contract with some awful magazine, promising that a reporter could come and live at the castle for a week at the end of this summer—next week, in fact—and write all about the life of the Earl of Lengroth.'

Heather blinked. Then she sat back, taking those beautiful breasts with her.

'But *Ryan's* the Earl. He can't have some reporter following him around for a week! He's *nine*!'

'Which is why I've spent the last five weeks in legal wrangling with their contracts team.' Cal sighed. 'I can't get us out of it. Trust me, Heather, I've given it everything I can. But the reporter is coming here next week—unless I hand over an absurd kill fee for the story *and* resign myself to them writing about us anyway, since apparently my brother was incapable of reading a contract.'

Maybe he'd been drunk at the time. Or just really, really desperate.

'Why would Ross have agreed to something like that? I mean, I know he'd have thought it would be *him* the reporter would be following around when he signed up for it, but still… I can't imagine anyone would want their lives being scrutinised that closely.'

Heather shuddered at the very idea. Cal didn't blame her.

'I've been trying to figure out the same thing myself. Ross was in debt, and in trouble with some…unsavoury people—so it could just have been that he needed the cash. Or…'

'Or…?' Heather prompted.

She'd shifted again, so she sat opposite him, cross-legged on the rug, and Cal found his gaze drawn to her stomach. Was that just the tiniest hint of rounding…the start of a baby bump there?

Cal sighed. That baby was coming, whatever happened, and it would be welcomed and loved. There was nothing Ross could do about that now.

'Or because he wanted to put on a show. I think... I think that maybe rumours were starting. That people were beginning to talk about him and his behaviour. The Bryce family rule has always been to keep trouble away from Lengroth, but there were enough people locally that Ross owed money to, or who had seen something. People might have been asking questions...'

'You think he was bringing the reporter here to show how perfect and scandal-free Lengroth Castle was?' Heather asked incredulously.

Cal shrugged. 'It's the family way. But now...'

'Now this reporter—'

'Anna Jenkins,' Cal supplied helpfully.

'Now Anna Jenkins is going to arrive to find Ross's pregnant one-night stand looking after his orphaned children and carrying on with his brother on the floor of the study.'

'Basically?' Cal flashed her a smile. 'Yes.'

* * *

This was awful. This was worse than awful. It was potentially front-page news for all the tabloids and gossip rags in the country. It was basically Heather's worst nightmare—and her father's, too.

And the worst part of all was that it didn't make her want Cal any less.

'So what do we do?' she asked, helplessness filling her.

The expression on Cal's face matched the way she felt. 'I guess we carry on as we were. Pretending that this—' he motioned to the air between them '—isn't there.'

Because that had been working *so* well for them before…

'For ever?'

'Hell, no.' Cal swore, and then crossed the space that had opened up between them and pulled her back into his arms. 'I can't keep my hands off you for that long. Even the next week is going to be a struggle, to be honest.'

Relieved, Heather snuggled into his embrace. 'So once the reporter has gone, then…?'

Cal nodded slightly—a gesture she felt rather

than saw, since his chin was tucked over her head. 'Just another week. Well, eight days. Then we'll talk, figure this out together. What we're going to do next and everything. I... Heather, I don't know what this is between us. But I want to at least give us a chance to find out.'

She nodded. 'Me, too. I mean, if my baby is going to know his half-brother and sister, then we can't screw this up.'

Desperate desire was one thing. But they needed still to be able to be friends when that faded.

If it faded.

That seemed pretty impossible right now.

She clenched her jaw and forced herself to push aside the thoughts that had been crowding her head since Cal had first kissed her. The thoughts that told her she was getting into something far deeper and far more dangerous than just a fling with her boss, or Ross's brother.

She was falling in love.

Heather knew better than to expect too much from Cal in the way of emotion. Lust he understood, clearly, but this was the man who hadn't even known how to love his niece and nephew. Expecting any romantic declarations from him was a disaster waiting to happen.

But even knowing that that wasn't enough to scare her off.

She'd deal with it all later, Heather decided. Her growing feelings for Cal could wait. There were too many other pressing things to worry about right now. Like the baby. Daisy and Ryan. Boarding school. The castle. The world... Not to mention her own future, her dad, her job, her home...

She should be using this time to plan, to figure out what the right thing to do by everybody was. But instead all she could think was *Eight days is too long.*

Far too long.

Pulling back ever so slightly, and feeling Cal's arms tightening around her automatically as she did so, Heather tilted her head to meet his gaze.

'She's not here until Monday?' she asked.

After all, today was only Saturday.

Cal nodded, apparently unable to look away from her eyes.

She knew how he felt. Whatever had brought her to Lengroth Castle in the first place, she knew that it was Cal who was going to keep her there. The thread that joined them now was too strong for her even to imagine it breaking.

'Not until Monday...' Cal repeated, his words barely a whisper.

'Then maybe we don't need to worry about what she or anyone else will think just yet.'

Heather pushed herself up until her lips brushed against Cal's again—the lightest feather touch, just a hint of what they could have.

Cal's eyes fluttered closed as he swallowed. 'You are temptation incarnate.'

'I thought you Bryce men liked that sort of thing?'

His eyes flashed open again, and the depth of lust and want in his amber eyes caught her by surprise.

'Oh, we do,' he said, with a wicked grin.

And then he kissed her again, and Heather decided to stop *thinking* about the right thing to do for a while and just *do* it instead.

* * *

Later—much later—Heather kissed Cal's bare shoulder and slipped out of his bed, her whole body still humming with pleasure.

'Where are you going?' Cal asked, his voice muffled by the duvet.

'Back to my room, before the kids wake up and come looking for me.'

Ryan in particular had developed a habit of waking her up by jumping on the end of her bed in the mornings. Heather quite liked it, really. It showed how comfortable he was with her now. But if she wasn't there when he came looking…

'Okay,' Cal said, pulling her back for another kiss all the same.

'Cal, I need to get back.'

He sighed, resting his forehead against her shoulder. 'I know. I just don't want to let you go when I've just got you here.'

She couldn't help but smile at that.

One last, swift kiss and she was on her way, padding down the stone corridors in bare feet, her shoes dangling from her fingers. The ultimate walk of shame, she supposed.

Suddenly she blinked as a figure appeared at the end of the corridor. Too tall for Daisy or Ryan, she realised quickly.

'Mrs Peterson?' she called, trying to smile.

The old housekeeper would expect an explanation, and Heather wasn't sure she had one just yet. She was a terrible liar, apart from anything else.

But then the figure turned, and although Heather couldn't quite make out her face she knew in her bones that it wasn't Mrs Peterson.

It wasn't anyone living at all.

Then the Lengroth ghost disappeared as quickly as she'd appeared, leaving Heather shivering in the stone-walled passageway of the castle, hoping this wasn't some sort of sign of things to come.

Cal stood at the top of the stone steps, scowling at the woman climbing out of Lengroth's only taxi down by the castle gates. She wasn't even fully on the premises yet and already he found himself hoping that Daisy might throw something at Anna the journalist.

Except no. Because that would look bad in the magazine.

Cal rubbed a hand over the back of his neck, squinted in the early-morning sunshine and tried one last time to think of a way out of this. Or at least to shake his foul mood.

He failed on both counts.

It was even more annoying because he'd been in *such* a good mood yesterday. Even waking up without Heather had been okay, because he'd known he'd have her back in his bed that night. Back in his arms, where she belonged.

Except then he'd remembered about the cursed Anna and her stupid magazine, and realised that he now wouldn't get to touch Heather again until the castle was journalist-free—a week from now.

A whole week.

He wasn't going to make it.

He knew it had been a bad idea to give in to the temptation of Heather's lips, her hands, her body. Because the problem with temptation was that once you'd given in the first time, the second was so much easier…

Cal was so lost in thought, remembering that

one perfect night with Heather, that he almost failed to notice that the smart brunette was making her way up the castle steps.

She was dressed in a suit that was worlds away from Heather's sundress and woolly cardigan wardrobe choices, and he couldn't help but think that Anna Jenkins was all wrong for this castle. Maybe she'd have fitted right in when Ross had been the Earl—he'd always been smartly dressed himself, and Janey had had exquisite fashion sense—but now that Ryan was in charge—and by extension Cal—standards had definitely slipped.

Hell, if it was hot enough they were lucky if they got Ryan into more than a pair of boxers some days—especially in the playroom, where the sun streamed through the large windows onto the window seat.

He'd have to remind Heather to try and keep him fully dressed...

'Lord Bryce.' Anna smiled brightly as she made her way up the seventeen stone steps, one tentative high-heeled foot at a time.

'Just Cal, please,' he said, reaching out a hand to her—partly for shaking, partly to make sure she didn't fall into the moat. 'My nephew is the Earl, not me.'

'So what does that make *you*, exactly?'

Anna's smile was shark-white, with every bit as much bite, as she took his hand. Her palm felt cool and dry, despite the morning sun, and it slid away from his almost as soon as they touched.

'It makes me Ryan's uncle.' Cal stepped back into the castle, holding the door open for her.

Already she was angling for the story she wanted to write, he realised. She must have been thrilled when Ross had died. An ordinary earl giving a magazine this kind of access was opportunity enough. But a child aristocrat with only an uncle for support, until recently absent? That was far more interesting.

Well, if she was hoping for resentment and jealousy on his part she was out of luck. He'd never wanted to be the Earl of Lengroth for a moment. He just hoped she didn't find anything more interesting to write about.

'Come on in,' he said, as pleasantly as he could. 'I'll introduce you to our housekeeper,

Mrs Peterson. She'll show you around the castle and get you settled in your room.'

At the far end of the castle, away from the children and Heather by design, even if it put her rather closer to his office than Cal would have liked.

'The housekeeper?' Anna's perfectly curved eyebrows arched just a little higher. 'Really, I'd love it if *you* could show me around yourself, Cal.'

'Unfortunately I have work to be getting on with. But here's Mrs Peterson now.'

Right on cue, the housekeeper arrived, resplendent in her best blue suit and pearls.

'And she'll introduce me to your niece and nephew?' Anna pressed.

Cal shook his head. 'I'm afraid the children are out on a day trip with their nanny. You'll meet them at dinner.'

A look of annoyance flashed across Anna's face.

Cal couldn't really blame her—but that didn't mean he was going to change his tactics. He and Heather had a plan, developed in the dark of night, curled up together in his bed. It was simple. Keep the reporter as far away from the children—and from Heather—for as much of her visit as possible. Mrs Peterson would handle the history of the castle and the family and so on, using the usual sanitised version, and Cal would do a proper interview—enough to keep her happy.

They'd fulfil the letter of the contract, but not the spirit. Because there was no way in hell Cal was allowing his nephew and niece to be exploited in some gossip magazine, however high-class the editor insisted it was.

And he wasn't letting Anna Jenkins find out about Heather and the baby, either.

Not if he could help it.

CHAPTER FOURTEEN

'HOW'S IT GONE TODAY?' Heather asked, slipping into Cal's office late on Thursday night.

His eyes widened. 'You shouldn't be here!'

Dropping into the chair opposite him, Heather rolled her eyes. 'Anna's already gone to bed for the night. Annoyed, according to Mrs Peterson. I do worry that if we frustrate her too much she'll go digging around for a scandal just to get back at us.'

For four days now Heather had kept the kids as far away from the castle as possible. There'd been picnics and day trips and long hikes— even a train ride into the city for the day. Anna had tried to suggest she accompany them on that one, but Cal had put on his best aristocratic voice and said, 'I thought you were here to cover life in the *castle*, Anna?' and that had been that.

Even Heather had been able to sense the journalist's annoyance although, as per the plan, she'd only seen her at breakfast and dinner each day. The children had stayed on their best behaviour for meals, answered Anna's questions in boring monotones, and basically helped create the impression that life at Lengroth Castle was nothing to write home about.

It was working, and Heather was glad.

But that did mean she'd barely seen Cal alone since the night she'd spent in his bed, and she missed him. More than she'd thought possible given that they were still living in the same castle.

'We just can't risk getting caught now, Heather. Not when we're so close to getting this over and done with.'

'I know,' Heather replied. 'I just…needed to see you.'

'I know the feeling,' Cal said, giving her a wry smile that reassured her he was suffering every bit as much as she was.

'I'll just sit here,' Heather promised. 'With a whole desk between us, getting into no trouble at all. We can talk about the children's educational progress, if you like.'

'Okay.' Cal sat back in his chair, arms folded across his chest. 'What have they learned this week?'

'Basically nothing—because we've been here there and everywhere, staying out of Anna's way.'

'Right. So we're done with that topic, then?'

Heather sighed. 'Cal…'

'I know. I know. I just… If you stay, I'm going to kiss you. I won't be able to help it. You're the ultimate temptation, and you know how bad the men in my family are at resisting that.'

'I do,' Heather agreed. 'But would it *really* be all that bad if you kissed me right now?'

She licked her lips. Her insides felt warmer just thinking about it. As if her blood was heating up inside her veins.

Cal's amber eyes darkened, and she knew he felt the same.

'Maybe not,' he said. 'But I wouldn't be able to stop at kissing you—you know that.'

'No?' Heather smiled dangerously. She knew this was a game they could ill afford to be playing right now, but maybe Cal wasn't the only one who had a problem with temptation. 'What else would you need to do?'

'*Need* is the right word,' Cal said, shifting in his seat. 'Because I need you so much right now, Heather. I need you naked on my desk. I need your skin against mine. I need you in my arms. I need—'

'I need you inside me again,' Heather interrupted, and Cal let out an honest-to-God growl at her words and got to his feet.

'You are going to be the death of me,' he said as he circled the desk and pulled her up out of her chair and into his arms—just where she wanted to be.

'Not just yet,' Heather said with a grin. 'I've got plans for you first.'

'Your room?' Cal asked.

'My room,' Heather confirmed. She was furthest away from Anna, and overwhelming lust hadn't completely dulled her good sense. *'Now.'*

It had just made her ignore it for a little while.

One more day. Tomorrow morning Anna would be on her way and the castle would be theirs again.

Theirs.

Not just his, or Ryan and Daisy's, but Heather's, too. Almost like a home.

When had *that* happened?

Long before he'd first taken Heather to bed, he knew. She belonged here—with them. The 'in his arms' part was purely for *his* benefit. And hers, he thought, smirking as he remembered leaving her breathless in bed that morning as he'd crept back to his own room before the rest of the castle awoke.

Heather might not stay for ever, but for now... she was everything he needed. Until the absurd levels of passion between them cooled he *had* to find a way to keep her at Lengroth. Otherwise he was honestly afraid he might go insane with want and need.

They were risking a lot, he knew. This last week had given him a far greater understanding of his ancestors than he'd ever expected to have. He'd always avoided any kind of personal risk—even the sort of risk Ross had apparently been addicted to as he'd gambled away his inheritance. But now... His whole world could go up in flames and as long as he could have Heather with him he wouldn't care.

He almost didn't recognise the person he'd become in the last six weeks. But that didn't mean he didn't like him.

'You're in a good mood this morning.'

Anna's sharp tones rang through the corridor and Cal looked up suddenly to find her standing in his way.

'It's a beautiful day,' Cal said, before glancing out of the window to see that rain clouds were gathering. Summer in Scotland. He supposed they'd been lucky to get away with as much good weather as they'd had that week. It would make it trickier for Heather to get the kids out of the castle today, though.

Anna followed his gaze to the window. 'I suppose summer means something rather different in Scotland to the rest of the country,' she said scathingly.

'You must be in a good mood, too,' Cal replied, falling into step with her as they headed for the dining room. 'You get to go home tomorrow.'

That was putting *him* in a very good mood, anyway.

'And leave all this splendour?' Anna replied, waving an arm towards the long dining table, loaded with Ryan's favourite sugary cereals and half a *pain au chocolat* left on Daisy's plate.

'Not what you expected from an earl's castle, huh?' Cal asked, hiding a smile.

Anna smiled back, but there was no warmth in it. 'Not exactly. I *would* like to get one last interview with you and the children before I leave, however.'

Cal glanced up to see Heather coming in from the kitchen. Meeting her eye, he knew she'd heard Anna's question. She gave a small, reluctant nod.

'I'm sure that can be arranged,' he told Anna, hoping she hadn't clocked the exchange. 'As long as I'm in the room with the children.'

'Of course.' Anna smiled sweetly, then made her way to a seat at the far end of the table.

Heather, Cal noticed, didn't look at all reassured by her promise.

'So, Heather, what do you and the children have planned for today?'

Heather met his eye before answering. He gave her what he hoped was an encouraging smile, rather than an *I want to ravish you on the breakfast table* smile, but really it could have gone either way.

'Since it looks like it's going to be a soggy day out there, I think we'll work on our history projects in the schoolroom today.'

'They're studying the Second World War,' Cal put in, as Daisy and Ryan both groaned in unison. He silenced them with a glare.

'You take a strong interest in your niece and nephew's education, then?' Anna commented, looking between them.

'Of course,' Cal said, surprised. 'And Miss Reid is excellent at keeping me updated on their progress.'

'I'm sure she is.'

Anna gave Heather a speculative look, and Cal suddenly regretted drawing attention to her. Still, they were nearly out of the woods. Just one more day and then Anna would be back on the early train to London, and he and Heather could sit down and figure out what happened next.

Preferably naked.

Heather was halfway through gluing a cardboard evacuee's suitcase together, while Ryan held the sides and Daisy found vital things to put in it when it was dry, when Mrs Peterson knocked on the schoolroom door.

'Miss Reid?'

The housekeeper had the same, slightly disapproving look on her face that she'd had ever since Heather had arrived at Lengroth Castle. The only slight consolation was that the look Mrs Peterson gave Anna Jenkins was even more scathing.

'Mr Bryce is looking for you.'

'He is?' Heather got to her feet. 'Keep holding that, Ryan, I'll be back in a moment.'

What on earth could Cal want? They'd agreed that they needed to stay away from each other as much as possible during the day while Anna was roaming the castle. At night it was a different matter. The only person likely to see

Heather then was apparently the Lengroth ghost—and even she'd been absent since that first night Heather had spent with Cal.

Heather knocked on the office door lightly, then let herself in.

Cal looked up from his computer screen with surprise. 'Heather! What's wrong? Do you need something?'

'I thought *you* did.' Heather frowned. 'Mrs Peterson said you were looking for me. Which I thought was strange because you knew exactly where I'd be...'

Their eyes met and they both reached the same conclusion at the same time.

'Anna!' they said, in unison.

'Your stupid castle is too big,' Heather muttered as they hurried down the endless stone-walled corridors back to the schoolroom.

'Yes, it's definitely the *castle* that's the problem here,' Cal replied, striding ahead. 'And it's not *my* castle. It's Ryan's.'

Ryan.

Ryan and Daisy—who were probably being cornered by that shark of a reporter right now, being asked heaven only knew what about their lives, their family, their parents' deaths—maybe even Cal and Heather.

Thank goodness they'd held back on telling them about the baby. Heather dreaded to think what Anna would have made of *that*.

Still, Heather's heart pounded as they rounded the final corner to the schoolroom and heard Anna's voice from inside.

'And how do you both feel about being sent away to boarding school by your uncle so soon after your parents' deaths?' she asked, her tone sweet but her words sharp.

Cal pushed past her to get inside, obviously not wanting to hear the answer to that one. But he wasn't as fast as Ryan's mouth.

'We're not going,' Ryan said defiantly. 'Heather would *never* let Uncle Cal send us away from Lengroth.'

Cal froze in front of her and Heather could almost hear his heart beating too fast, too hard, at his nephew's words.

'Do you think your nanny has that sort of influence?' Anna asked. 'I thought she was only here for the summer...'

'Heather's not just the nanny,' Daisy replied,

her tone scathing. 'She's pregnant with Daddy's baby. And Uncle Cal is in love with her.'

'So she's going to stay for ever and we'll all be a family again!' Ryan shouted. 'You'll see!'

CHAPTER FIFTEEN

RYAN PUSHED PAST Anna and ran out through the schoolroom doorway—and barrelled right into Cal, who pulled him into a hug, holding the boy's trembling body against his chest.

Behind him, Heather slumped back against the wall, and he didn't need to look at her to know that she had to be looking as stunned as he felt.

How did they find out about the baby?

A question for later. Once he'd dealt with the enormous problem directly at hand.

'I think it's time you left Lengroth Castle, Miss Jenkins,' he said over Ryan's head, his tone icy.

In one short minute Daisy and Ryan had destroyed generations worth of the careful deceit and lies protecting the Bryce family's reputation. All the work he'd been doing to keep

Ross's infidelities and gambling a secret was pointless now.

But, worst of all, they'd exposed Heather to gossip and scandal, too.

'My train isn't until tomorrow,' Anna said.

'It's a long walk to the station,' Cal replied. 'Go. Now.'

Her eyes widened as she looked up at him, and whatever she saw in his expression obviously convinced her, because she scuttled past him down the corridor. He'd have to deal with her again eventually, Cal knew—if only to find out what and when her magazine would be printing in order to do some damage limitation. But that would have to wait.

First he needed to take care of Daisy and Ryan. And Heather.

He glanced over his shoulder, looking for a moment of solidarity with Heather before he dealt with the children, but she was gone. The corridor was empty. And Cal felt a sneaking feeling of dread working its way towards his heart.

'Uncle Cal is in love with her!'

That was what Ryan had said. Obviously that was crazy, but did Heather know that?

'Uncle Cal?' Daisy's voice wobbled as she spoke, and Cal spun back to face her. 'Are we in trouble?'

Time slowed and stilled as his niece's question echoed in his brain. He knew instantly what his father's reaction would have been—and his father's father's. He'd lived it once. Never on this scale, but with an unguarded comment at a dinner party that had resulted in a broken arm, or a conversation with Harry at school that had ended with Cal being thrashed after someone had started asking questions.

He could never know how Ross might have handled this moment with his children. But he knew how *he* wanted to handle it. And he knew why.

He looked between Daisy and Ryan and realised that whatever happened next it had all been worth it. Because right now, in this moment, he found himself reaching for a truth he'd believed would always be beyond him.

He wasn't angry. He didn't want to shout.

Even with everything that was at stake his only concern was protecting the children.

Because he loved them.

Against all the odds, he loved them.

'You're not in trouble, either of you.' He held an arm out towards Daisy and pulled her into his embrace along with her brother. 'I want to talk to you about what you both said, but I promise you this—you're not in trouble. I love you both, and nothing either one of you could ever do could possibly change that.'

The force of his words filled him as his niece and nephew clung to his shirt, which was suddenly suspiciously damp in places. Daisy would never admit to crying, but Cal didn't need her to. He'd done what he'd thought was impossible.

He, a Bryce male, had found a way to love his children—*his*, now Ross was gone. And *his* in his heart.

He wouldn't inflict the cycle of lies and secrets upon Daisy and Ryan. They'd spoken the truth—however they'd learned it—or the truth as they saw it. He couldn't be angry with them for that, whatever the consequences.

Heather had been right when she'd told him that it wasn't the scandal and people's actions that hurt the most. It was the secrets and the lies people told to keep their misdeeds from seeing the light of the day.

Which meant that the only way out of this was to tell the truth.

All of it.

However terrifying that was.

But first he needed to take care of Daisy and Ryan.

'Come on,' he said. 'Let's go find some hot chocolate and talk about all this. I have some questions—and I'm sure you both do, too. And questions always go better with chocolate.'

That sounded like something Heather would say. Heather, who had given him all this. Heather, whose smile lit him up from the inside and whose body against his had made everything feel real and right for the first time in his life.

Heather, whom he wanted to protect and care for, just as much as he did the children. Heather, who was carrying another child that he wanted to be a part of their family.

Heather, who…

Oh, hell. Ryan was right.

Except Heather was missing in action right now, so there wasn't anything he could do about his realisation except stamp it down to deal with later. The children came first, and without Heather there to help this was all on him.

For the first time he felt as if he was equal to the challenge.

Heather stared at the rucksack on her bed, filled with only the things she'd brought with her when she'd arrived at Lengroth Castle. She couldn't take any of the things Cal had bought her. Not now.

It looked strangely empty, though.

She should have left already. She should have run the moment that Anna had gone from the castle. How could she stay now all their secrets were out?

Cal had spent a lifetime keeping his family's secrets—and his forebears had been doing it for much longer. And she… She'd worked so hard always to do the right thing, never to make her father worry, never to bring gossip and talk to his door—until this year.

This year she'd thrown caution to the wind—twice—and given up everything she'd fought for since her mother had left in her own cloud of disgrace.

The moment Anna published news of the Lengroth scandal—online or in print—Heather's name would be out there. And so would her misdeeds.

She had to get home to her father and tell him before he heard it from someone else. But she had to talk to Cal first. Which was why she was still standing there, staring at a half-empty rucksack as if it reflected her own half-empty heart.

'The kids are in bed.'

Cal's quiet voice behind her made her jump. She spun to see him standing in the open doorway, leaning against the doorframe, his amber eyes watchful.

'I'm sorry. I should have stayed with you. But I needed to—'

'Pack,' Cal interrupted, his gaze flicking to the rucksack.

'Think,' she corrected. 'And I wasn't going to leave without talking to you first.'

'But you *are* going to leave.' His eyes weren't watchful any longer. They were hard. 'You said you weren't going to do that.'

Heather swallowed. 'My contract with you finishes next week anyway. You're sending the kids away, remember?'

Cursing under his breath, Cal crossed the room and took her hands. 'Do you really think things are the same as they were at the start of this summer? Heather, *everything* has changed.'

'Does that mean you're going to pay me anyway? Even if I leave a few days early?' she joked, but Cal didn't seem to find it funny.

'You can take all the money you want if you're insisting on leaving. I'd hoped… I'd thought we could talk tonight. Come up with a plan for what happens next.'

Heather gave a small bitter laugh. 'We both heard what Ryan and Daisy said to Anna. I think we *know* what happens next. The whole country finds out that I slept with a married man, got knocked up from my one-night stand with him, then came here to seduce his brother and win over his other kids. My father will spiral into despair at my actions, and I will become an absolute outcast and a scandal.'

She'd seen it before. Her mother would have been forced to leave the village in the end—even if she hadn't taken off with her lover. It would have become untenable for her to stay.

Just as it was for Heather now.

'It doesn't have to be that way,' Cal offered.

Heather shook her head. 'You know better than that, Cal. How can I walk into Lengroth with Daisy and Ryan now, with everyone knowing who I am and what I've done?'

'With me at your side,' Cal said, squeezing her hands as he dropped to one knee. 'Heather, stay here and marry me.'

A chill swept through Heather as if the Lengroth ghost had walked right through her. That poor woman who'd been knocked up by the old Earl and murdered when she'd tried to tell the truth about it.

Now here was Cal, offering her everything that any woman could have wanted—and Heather knew she couldn't take it.

'I can't—' Her voice broke on the words.

'Why?' Cal didn't move from his knee. 'We can make this work, Heather—you've taught me that. You've taught me that I *can* love, even if my parents never could. I know I can do this now—be a parent to Ryan and Daisy, love them the way they need to be loved. And if I can do that maybe I can even have a happy marriage— as long as it's with *you*. You've shown me that it's not always what we do that hurts others, it's the secrets we keep. So I'm not going to keep secrets any more. I'm going to shout the truth from the turrets of this cursed castle.'

He swallowed so hard she saw his throat bob, then he held her gaze with his own as he spoke.

'I'm going to tell the world that I love you. Starting with you. Heather Reid, I'm in love with you—and I need you to stay.'

Oh, God, his words were arrows through her heart. She knew how much those words must have cost him. How hard he'd fought to be able even to *think* them, let alone say them. And she wasn't even going to try to deny any longer that she was just as much in love with him.

But it didn't matter.

She couldn't live this life.

Couldn't stay here with everyone—even Daisy and Ryan—knowing what sort of a person she was. With her *child* knowing.

'What about Anna?' she asked, her mouth dry.

Cal smiled, obviously taking her question as agreement. 'I've already called Anna's magazine and offered them a proper interview about it all with a different journalist if they don't print Anna's piece. We can announce our engagement, explain our side of the story. It'll all blow over in no time.'

But it wouldn't. People in her village still talked about her mother's misdeeds now, eighteen years or more later. Nobody would forget what she'd done, either—and, most of all, *she* wouldn't forget.

She'd done the wrong thing—sleeping with a married man, falling for Cal, lying about it all.

She didn't deserve a happy-ever-after here.

But her child did.

And she was going to make sure he or she got it.

Even if it broke her heart.

* * *

This was all going to work out. All she had to do was say yes and he could fix everything— just as he'd been fixing things ever since he'd returned to Lengroth Castle. With Heather at his side he could do it all.

Except she wasn't saying yes.

'I'm sorry, Cal. I can't marry you.'

He could *see* the pain in her eyes, hear her voice cracking. He knew she wanted this every bit as much as he did. He didn't need her to say the words. He could feel it between them whenever they were together. Hell, she'd probably known he loved her before *he* did. They'd both just pushed everything aside to deal with later.

But she wanted them to be a family. She wanted *him*. So why wouldn't she say yes?

'I'm not doing this because it will avoid a scandal. I'm doing this because I love you.'

It was possibly the first time anyone in his family had *ever* proposed purely for love. Janey had been pregnant when Ross had put a ring on her finger, and Cal was pretty sure he wouldn't have if their father hadn't insisted.

And Heather was turning him down.

'I know. I know. And I love you, too. I tried not to, but…'

There were tears in her eyes, he realised.

Cal pulled himself up to stand, tugging her closer as he did so. 'You love me, Heather. And I love you. So to hell with everyone else. Marry me, make us a real family and let us be happy together.'

She met his gaze, eyes gleaming. 'I want to. But I won't do that to my child. I won't let my child grow up here, where people will always talk about us. Where his or her whole life will be defined by what I did before he or she was even born. I grew up like that, Cal, and I can't do it to my baby. However much I love you, I love my baby more.'

His hands fell away from hers without his permission and he stepped back without planning to. It seemed his body had accepted what she was saying even if his heart hadn't.

'What about Daisy and Ryan? I thought you loved them, too.'

'I do,' she said, her voice pained. 'But they have you—and you have them. I know the three of you can be a happy family together. And it will be easier for you without me and my scandal hanging over you.'

'*Nothing* will be easier without you,' Cal replied, his temper rising.

But Heather only shook her head. As if the matter was out of her hands. But it wasn't. His whole future was in her hands.

'You're running scared,' he accused her. 'I always thought that *I* was the one too scared of repeating the past to risk falling in love, to try to be part of a functioning happy family. But *you're* the one who told me that I could— that kids need love more than perfection. More than *anything* else. Well, the same goes for me. I need your love—not for you to be perfect, or scandal-free.'

'You might not say that when people start talking.'

'I will. I know I will. Because you've made me believe it—made me believe that I can change my family legacy. But you won't even take a chance on changing yours.'

'I *can't*, Cal.'

His heart breaking, Cal tried one last time. 'You say you're doing this for your baby, to make things easier for Daisy and Ryan and even me. But what about *you*? What about what you want?'

With a sad smile Heather picked up the rucksack from her bed. 'I don't deserve what I want.'

And then she walked out of the room, the castle and his life—like the ghost he wasn't even sure existed.

CHAPTER SIXTEEN

THE TRAIN RIDE home was miserable.

Even in summer the sleeper train from Edinburgh to London was freezing, and Heather's coat barely kept her warm enough to stop her shivering. Tears leaked constantly from her eyes, chilling her cheeks, but she couldn't have stopped them if she'd tried.

She'd left her heart, maybe even her soul, in Lengroth Castle, and she had no idea if she'd ever get them back again.

But the train wasn't the worst part. The worst part was telling her father everything.

It took her four days to pluck up the courage, but in the end she knew she couldn't wait any longer if she wanted him to hear it from her instead of reading it in some magazine.

It was a miracle the news wasn't out there already—that or the fact that Cal had used the old Bryce magic to keep it hidden for now. But the truth would come out in the end. Even the truth about her feelings for Cal, which she realised now she'd been denying for as long as she'd been feeling them.

Now her father sat opposite her, in the same armchair by the window that had been 'Dad's chair' her whole life, a cup of tea long gone cold at his elbow. She'd wanted to shield him from the worst of her actions, wanted to fudge the truth and skip over certain events.

But she hadn't been able to. She owed him the whole truth, however awful it was.

'And so you came back here?' her dad asked eventually, after she'd finished.

'Yes.'

Her dad reached for a biscuit from the plate on the coffee table.

'I can leave if you want,' Heather said. 'I mean, I know this is going to be a big story. It'll probably make the papers. And I'll totally understand if you want me far away when that happens. I was thinking maybe I could rent a cottage somewhere in Wales—like where we used to go on holiday. Take some time away from everything.'

Before she'd even reached London there had been a full year's wages sitting in her bank account. Cal had been as good as his word—even when she hadn't. He'd given her the means to take time to figure out what to do next, and she could never thank him enough for that.

Maybe she'd send him a postcard from Wales. If he ever wanted to hear from her again, that was.

'Or you could go back to Scotland right now,' her dad said, and Heather started, staring at him in confusion.

'You…you really want me to go?'

She'd said she'd understand it if he did, but when it came to it she'd hoped her father would support her. And why would she run away to *Scotland*, of all places?

Her dad slipped his glasses from his nose, folded them, then placed them on the table next to his cold tea—a gesture so familiar that it made Heather's heart ache for the time before this summer. Before she'd ever met Ross Bryce, when life had been simple, ordered and safe.

'Heather. Sweetheart. I will love you and support you your whole life—whatever you choose to do, and whatever mistakes you make. And you will always have a home here.'

'Thank you,' Heather whispered, her eyes burning with more tears that wouldn't fall.

'But I'm your father, and it's my job to tell you when I think you're making a mistake. And I don't mean getting pregnant by an earl, or running away and not telling me. I mean leaving Cal and those two children up there in Lengroth.'

Heather blinked. 'I'm sorry...?'

Sighing, her dad reached forward to take her hands—a reassuring gesture that reminded her so much of Cal that her heart ached anew.

'You love that man, *and* those children—even I can see that, just hearing you talking about them. Not to mention how miserable you've been since you arrived home. So you need to go back and be with them.'

'But—'

Her father put up a hand to stop her. 'No buts. Whatever reasons you've dreamed up to keep you apart from them, I guarantee they're not good enough. When your mother left...'

'Dad, you don't have to talk about this.' He never had—not once before. She didn't want to think about how miserable she must look to make him want to talk about it now.

'Yes, I do. Because you need to understand. When she left…she took my heart with her. All the talk, all the gossip…it hurt, of course it did. But not because of what other people thought about me, or my marriage. It was because every single word was a reminder that she didn't love me the way I'd loved her, the way she'd said she did, right until that last day. Worse—it was a reminder that she didn't even love *you* enough to stay. And that was the part I just couldn't make sense of. Because you are the best thing in my life, and I don't understand how anyone could walk away from you.'

'Dad…'

'I'm not finished. Because if your Cal feels about you half the way you feel about him… I imagine he's in a lot of pain right now. Just like I was.'

I need your love—not for you to be perfect, or scandal-free.

Oh, God, what if he'd really meant that? And what if…what if that was all her baby needed, too?

Two parents who loved him or her. A family to be part of.

Cal might not be her child's biological father, but she knew he'd be his or her dad in his heart, just as he would for Daisy and Ryan.

'I always thought… I thought it was the scandal that broke you. I spent my whole life trying to avoid bringing that kind of talk to your door again.'

Had it all been for nothing? No. Because it had made her the person she was. The person who'd trekked all the way to Lengroth to do 'the right thing'.

The person Cal had fallen in love with.

Cal had loved Ross—loved him still, despite all his flaws. And he loved her, too. Maybe as much as she loved him.

'I can take any words any person throws at me,' her dad said softly. 'But I can't take my only daughter, the love of my life, being unhappy when she doesn't need to be.'

Heather fell to her knees in front of his chair, letting her father wrap his arms around her as she sobbed into his lap. And when at last she was all out of tears, he helped her to her feet and said, 'Grab your bag. I'll take you back to the station.'

'What are you going to do now?'

Cal looked up as Mrs Peterson placed a cup of hot chocolate on the table in front of him, then added a tumbler of brandy beside it. She'd been apologetic and full of guilt ever since she'd realised that Anna had tricked her into getting the children alone so she could interrogate them.

'What *can* I do? I'll call Anna's editor again—manage the story as well as I can now it's out there. I've already paid Heather what I owed her, so that's sorted. Next I'll call the boarding school and—'

'And what?' Daisy's voice rang out from the kitchen door, where she stood with her pale hair hanging around her face and her pyjamas hanging off her slim frame. 'Do we have to go? Now that Heather isn't here?'

Telling the kids she was gone had been awful.

Daisy had pretended she didn't care, of course, but Ryan had sobbed, and Cal had known that Daisy was lying, so that wasn't any easier. They couldn't understand why she'd gone if it wasn't because she was cross with them, and Cal hadn't been able to explain because he didn't understand either.

He knew her reasons. But he couldn't understand them.

He'd always assumed that when it came to relationships it would be him who couldn't make it work. Who pulled back for fear of the world learning the truth about his family, or because he really was a product of his gene pool and incapable of true love.

But in the end he'd overcome all that—and it still hadn't been enough.

He'd felt those old walls and old beliefs rising up again that night when Heather had left. But in the morning Daisy and Ryan had been there, a constant reminder of why he had to fight to be more than his own father had been. Why love mattered even when it hurt.

'What do you and Ryan *want* to do?' Cal asked, realising belatedly that he had never asked them. 'Go to Derryford or stay here with me, even if Heather isn't here? You'd have to go to the village school, but I always quite liked it there.'

'Stay at Lengroth,' Daisy said promptly. 'Ryan would be miserable away from Lengroth. And besides, I think you need us.'

Cal smiled. 'I think I do, too. Well, that's decided, then.'

And with that one thing sorted, things began to fall into place.

Anna's editor wasn't exactly accommodating now there were no engagement photos to publish, but eventually they reached an agreement. He refused to let Anna back into the castle, but did submit to a lengthy, open and honest phone interview with one of her colleagues, and agreed that they could use the photos Anna had taken at Lengroth.

People were still going to talk. A lot. But Cal didn't care. The truth was the truth, and lying about it wouldn't change it.

He did have to sit down with Daisy and Ryan and tell them everything, however, in the most age-appropriate way he could manage. Apparently they were far better eavesdroppers than he'd given them credit for—as was Mrs Peterson. And the housekeeper had been far less discreet than he'd hoped.

Which was another uncomfortable conversation he'd have to have…

Cal cornered the housekeeper who'd run Lengroth like clockwork since he was a child as she was making apple pie.

'When you called me the night Ross died you told me they were coming home from a party. But that was a lie, wasn't it?'

She shook the flour from her hands. 'It was.'

'Why?'

'Because that's what we do at Lengroth. We hide the things we don't want other people to see.'

'Not any more,' Cal said firmly. 'Sit down and tell me the truth.'

And she did. She told him about all the women Ross had paraded through the castle, right in front of his wife and children. About the late-night poker games when the attendees had ended up taking home precious heirlooms instead of the money Ross owed them.

'Why didn't you call me? Tell me what was happening?'

Mrs Peterson shrugged. 'He was the Earl.'

'And the night they died?'

'Janey lost her patience—finally. I don't know what it was that did it, but it could have been any one of a hundred things Ross did. She told him she was leaving—packed a bag and everything.'

'She didn't take the kids?'

'I think she knew that Ross wouldn't let her. And as the Earl he had more power. I don't know. I don't think she was thinking straight. They'd both been drinking, I know that.'

'So what happened?'

Mrs Peterson toyed with the apple peeler on the table. 'She got in the car, ready to drive away, but he forced his way into the passenger seat. Told her she couldn't go anywhere without him—people would talk. She drove off anyway. And that was the last time I ever saw them alive.'

Cal shuddered, thankful beyond belief that Janey hadn't tried to take the children. He might have lost everyone in one awful night, and all because Ross hadn't wanted the world to know that his wife was leaving him.

The magazine hit the stands the next day, with the article and photos already up on the website and gaining comments the night before. Cal woke that morning to a throng of reporters gathered around the gates, waiting for a comment.

'What do I do with them?' Mrs Peterson asked.

Cal shrugged. 'Offer them a cup of tea?'

He'd told the truth, answered the questions, and now it was up to others to think what they wanted about it.

Inside Lengroth Castle with Daisy and Ryan, his family, he felt safe and happy. Or as happy as he could be with a hole in his home where Heather should be.

'What are you going to do?' Mrs Peterson called after him.

'Talk to the kids about redecorating their rooms,' Cal answered over his shoulder.

It was time to bring some new life into the castle, he'd decided.

* * *

The reporters were still there the next day, too, happily munching the bacon butties Mrs Peterson had made them. Cal ignored them, looking at wallpaper and paint swatches with the kids in the playroom instead.

At least until Ryan looked out of the window and yelled, 'Look!'

Cal crossed to the window seat and looked. And then he smiled as, down below, Heather walked through the gates of Lengroth Castle, a rubber duck under her arm.

Heather had made it all the way to Scotland before anyone had recognised her from the magazine photos, and even then they hadn't been too hard to put off. But here at Lengroth, with a crowd of reporters thronging around the main gate, there was no pretending to be anyone other than exactly who she was.

The pregnant one-night stand of the late Earl.

Or maybe the fiancée of the new Earl's uncle—if the offer still stood.

Climbing out of the taxi, Heather took a deep breath, adjusted the rubber duck she'd carried all the way from London King's Cross, and grabbed her bag.

'Good luck, Heather.' Harris the taxi driver threw her a grin. 'I reckon you'll all be fine now you're back.'

'I hope so. And thanks.'

Maybe this wouldn't be all bad.

'Heather! Heather!'

The reporters were calling her name before she even reached the gates. Heather ignored them—especially the ones calling out questions that asked her to 'compare and contrast' the two brothers.

Finally, as she opened the gate, she spun to face them. 'Thank you all for your interest,' she said, as they fell silent apart from the click of the odd camera shutter. 'But this is a family matter. And I'd like to get home to my family, please.'

If they'd still have her.

The questions and shouting started up again immediately, but Heather barely heard it. Because when she turned towards the castle again she saw Cal, standing at the top of the seventeen stone steps that led to the front door, waiting for her.

'I'm so sorry,' she said as she reached the first step.

'I thought you were never coming back.' Cal jumped down a few steps to meet her sooner, sweeping her into his arms as soon as she reached the middle step. 'I've never been so happy to be wrong.'

'Me, neither,' Heather admitted. 'I couldn't stay away. And my dad made me see that I shouldn't. I love you—and Daisy and Ryan. I belong here, and so does our baby.'

'Too right.' Cal kissed her, hard and deep, dipping her over his arm as a cheer went up from the reporters at the gate. 'Wait—*our* baby?'

'Our family, really, I thought. If you still want to marry me?'

'In a heartbeat,' Cal answered, and kissed her again.

This time, the cheer that went up was much closer, and Heather opened her eyes to find Daisy and Ryan watching from the doorway.

'You're *really* getting married?' Ryan asked.

'You're *staying* this time?' Daisy added.

Heather and Cal exchanged a glance.

'Yes, to both,' Heather said, smiling widely. 'Want to be bridesmaid?'

Daisy rolled her eyes. 'No. But I'll help you choose the food.'

'Even better.'

'Guess what, Heather!' Ryan grabbed her arm as he spoke. 'We're not going away to school! We're staying here.'

'I'm so glad,' Heather said. 'I'd have missed you too much if you'd gone.'

'We *all* missed *you*,' Cal said. 'So maybe it's best that we just stay together from now on—agreed?'

'A family?' Daisy asked tentatively. 'You two, us, Mrs Peterson and the baby?'

Behind them, Mrs Peterson looked surprised to be included—but Heather was almost certain she saw a tear in the housekeeper's eye.

'All of us,' Heather said firmly. 'Together.'

'Always,' Cal confirmed.

And as he spoke Heather could have sworn she saw another figure—a thin white figure, almost transparent in the late-summer sunshine—behind Mrs Peterson. A ghostly figure that raised a hand in farewell, then disappeared.

Heather lifted her own hand automatically, before realising there was no one there to see it. The Lengroth ghost had moved on at last. Maybe because the Bryce family no longer needed a reminder of the harm their misdeeds could cause, Heather thought with a smile.

Suddenly the whole castle felt lighter. As if years of secrets and lies had been lifted from the stones.

Heather gathered her family close and, with their arms around each other, they all headed into Lengroth Castle.

Together.

EPILOGUE

THE DARK METAL gates of Lengroth Castle were thrown open in the summer sunshine, and crowds of wedding guests were pouring through to celebrate with Heather and Uncle Cal on this glorious July day. Daisy watched them through the playroom window for a while, before deciding she probably had better put on her dress before Heather came looking for her.

It was, Daisy thought, exactly a year to the day since she'd thrown a rubber duck through that same window—the day Heather had arrived at Lengroth. She smiled to herself. Every table at the wedding breakfast had a rubber duck as part of its centrepiece—one wearing a top hat, another dressed as a centurion, a rubber duck sphinx and so on. Daisy didn't know where Heather had found them, but they were pretty funny.

Her dress wasn't too bad, either, Daisy thought as she put it on. Heather had let her choose—and had let her off bridesmaid duties, too, which Daisy was glad about. She didn't want everyone staring at her today. She wanted to sit with Ryan and Heather's dad—who had said to call him Grandpa Bill—and just enjoy it all.

Today, after all the awfulness of last year, they were going to be a family again.

And the new baby was cute. Daisy thought it was nice that they had someone they could all share, who belonged to all of them together.

Heather and Uncle Cal had called him Will, after her dad. Ryan had pointed out that it wasn't actually the same name. He cried a lot, but he always seemed to stop when Daisy sang him songs. In the end she and Ryan had decided that Will was better than a puppy—but they still kind of wanted a dog, too.

Uncle Cal had said they'd go and pick one after the honeymoon. Heather had given him a big kiss when he'd said that, which was strange, as Daisy hadn't thought Heather was really a dog person.

Checking her reflection in the mirror, Daisy saw a flicker of movement behind her and smiled. She knew who that was.

She turned slowly, so as not to spook the ghost, and then laughed at herself for being silly. Ghosts weren't scared of *people.*

Heather thought the ghost had left the day she'd come back to the castle, but Daisy knew better. Yes, she'd *mostly* gone, but every now and again, on important days, she came back—just to check on them. Daisy liked her. She was the only person she'd had to talk to, apart from Ryan, when her parents had died—and Ryan had been too little and too much of a boy to understand.

'Hello,' Daisy said. 'Have you come to check that we're still all right?'

The ghost nodded.

Daisy sat down on the bed to pull on her shiny silver shoes. 'We're fine. Better than fine, really. Don't tell anyone I said this, but Uncle Cal and Heather are getting really good at this

family thing. I still miss Mum and Dad but…
we're happy. All of us together. So you don't
need to worry any more.'

The ghost smiled. Daisy didn't think she'd
seen her do that before.

'Oh, and if you come to visit over the next
couple of weeks we won't be here,' Daisy added
quickly as the ghost started to fade. 'We're all
going on honeymoon together, you see. Uncle
Cal says it'll be more fun if we're together.
Mrs Peterson is coming, too—to help with the
baby.'

And, Daisy suspected, to let Uncle Cal and
Heather have some time alone. Really, she was
eleven now. She understood more than they
thought.

She wondered if maybe their family might
grow again soon. That would be okay, she decided. Especially if she got a dog, too.

'Daisy? Are you ready?' Heather appeared in
the doorway just as the ghost vanished completely. 'Oh, you look beautiful!'

'You look nice, too,' Daisy said.

It was true—Heather's copper hair was tied
up in some complicated plait at the back of her

head, and her dress was ivory lace and pearls. But mostly she just looked so happy it shone out of her.

'Shall we go and find the boys?' Heather asked, holding a hand out to Daisy. 'The sooner we get the wedding part over with, the sooner we can get to the dancing.'

Daisy rolled her eyes. Dancing was Heather's favourite thing about getting married, it seemed. 'Might as well.'

As they walked down the stone-floored hallways to the castle chapel Daisy thought she saw the ghost peeping out at them one last time.

'Heather? You'll never leave again, will you?'

When she'd first come back Daisy had asked her that every day—usually in a whisper at bedtime, so she could pretend she hadn't really said it. But now she hadn't asked her in months, she realised. Maybe because she already knew the answer. But it was still nice to hear it.

'Never,' Heather promised. 'Nothing could take me away from you and Ryan, or Will, or Uncle Cal.'

'Good.' Daisy sneaked a look back at the ghost, who smiled again, then disappeared.

Somehow Daisy didn't think she'd be back. The Bryce family didn't need watching over any more. Not now they had each other.

* * * * *